MAC WA]
40,000 I
(Mac Walke

By D.W. Ulsterman

2014

Other full length novels in the Mac Walker series:

MAC WALKER'S AMERICAN JIHAD
(Mac Walker #2)

MAC WALKER'S BENGHAZI
(Mac Walker #3)

MAC WALKER'S BETRAYAL
(Mac Walker #4)

DOMINATUS
(Mac Walker #5)

TUMULTUS
(Mac Walker #6)

http://ulstermanbooks.com/

Like us on Facebook at:

https://www.facebook.com/author.dwulsterman

NOTE FROM THE AUTHOR:

Greetings! If this is your first foray into the character of Mac Walker, I say welcome! And to those who are already well acquainted with Mr. Walker, I say welcome back!

Mac Walker's 40,000 Feet works as either a standalone novel, or as another integral chapter in the now six novel storyline of Mac Walker. Chronologically, this is the earliest telling of Mac Walker's story to date, coming before the events **of *Mac Walker's American Jihad*, *Mac Walker's Benghazi*, *Mac Walker's Betrayal*, *Dominatus*, and *Tumultus*.**

I also want to point out that an important character from ***Bennington P.I.: Take two and call me in the morgue"*** is also included in *40,000 Feet* – Father Victor Barnes. For those who, after reading *40,000 Feet* are intrigued by the character of Father Barnes, I suggest you give ***Bennington P.I.*** a look.

Until then, happy reading.

-D. W. Ulsterman

*He which hath no stomach to this fight,
Let him depart; his passport shall be made.*

-Henry V, Act IV

March 17th, 2002 – twenty minutes after take-off from Paris

1.

Mac Walker never was much for flying which was ironic given he found himself spending so much time doing just that. It wasn't fear of crashing that made him uncomfortable, so much as having to share such a confined space with so many other people. From the kid squalling behind him, to the young couple proving their lust for one another two rows in front, to the absurdly effeminate male flight attendant who kept walking past Mac's seat to look down at him with barely concealed lust.

Being a passenger on a plane, particularly a commercial flight where he had to sit closely with so many other people, had a way of creeping him out.

Wouldn't be so bad if I could just fly this thing myself. Close that cockpit door behind me and get on home in some peace and quiet.

Mac's seat moved forward several inches as the boy seated behind him, positioned his feet against the back of Mac's headrest. The just recently retired Navy SEAL closed his eyes and inhaled slowly as both of his hands dug into the soft vinyl armrests at either side of him.

Swear to God, I won't hurt that kid, but his pansy ass dad could sure use a good smack for letting him behave this way.

Mac opened his eyes to see the same male flight attendant coming his way, the man's eyes already devouring him hungrily with each step. The flight attendant, likely just a few years past thirty, was not quite six foot, with a thin build and short cut brown hair combed neatly to the right side of his head. He smiled down at Mac as he slowly walked by him, his eyes lingering for just a moment too long on Mac's crotch.

Ok, I won't hurt the kid, and I won't rage on the creepy flight attendant, but I still might smack the kid's dad – just because.

True to his intense military training and experience, the thirty eight year old Mac Walker had already initiated a mental inventory of every seat surrounding him prior to taking his own. Each face was filed away into his short term memory. He knew the exact distance to the emergency exits, and had already begun to note the timing of the airline staff's in-flight routines.

It was during that mental inventory Mac Walker noticed the occupant in the right side aisle seat five rows up from him. The man was mid-forties, at least six foot, slightly overweight, with a large, dark and gray mustache that hung to the sides of his mouth. Mac watched intently as the man did his own inventory of the flight's current occupants. That piqued the former Navy SEAL's interest, but it was how the man sat in his seat leaning slightly to the right that confirmed for Mac who the man was.

Air marshal.

The air marshal likely had his weapon holstered under his jacket on his left side, which made it somewhat uncomfortable for him to sit squarely in his seat. The presence of air marshals on U.S. flights had become increasingly common following 9-11. The American government had initiated a fast-track in-the-air training program for thousands of law enforcement personnel, and Mac Walker was certain Mr. Mustache was one of those.

"Oh, I hate it when the clouds make it so you can't see outside."

Mac glanced to his left where an older woman was staring out the small window next to her, silently giving thanks that an empty seat separated them. Not that he had anything against old women mind you, it just meant more elbow room, and that helped to make the eight hour flight almost bearable.

The woman turned to look at Mac, wanting to make sure he heard her. She had a friendly, grandmotherly face that reminded Mac of a somewhat older version of his own mother back home in Carville, Louisiana.

"Do you think those clouds will go away?"

Mac offered a quick half smile back at the older woman as he too peeked through the window at the white mass of swirling moisture that enveloped the still climbing 767.

"We should be above the cloud cover soon, ma'am. I'd guess another ten minutes or so."

The woman's face broke out into a wide smile, revealing a brilliant white row of dentures.

"You're American, a Southerner?"

"Yes ma'am, Louisiana born and raised.

The woman's right hand reached across the empty seat and placed itself gently on Mac's left forearm as she leaned over closer to him.
"That must be where you get your good manners. Don't get so much of that anymore these days – young men don't seem to know how to behave properly."

As she spoke those last words the woman's eyes glared behind her where the young boy was now making a series of loud and quite obnoxious farting noises while his father pretended not to notice.

Mac nodded his head briefly.

"Well, I had parents who cared enough and weren't shy about letting me know when wrong was wrong."

The older woman smiled again, her warm blue eyes looking at Mac approvingly.

"My name is Eldra Peabody. It's very nice to meet you."

Mac carefully shook Eldra's heavily knuckled right hand lightly, sensing she suffered from arthritis.

"Thank you, Eldra. My name is Mac – Mac Walker. Hey, look outside there."

Eldra turned to the window where she was greeted by flashes of brilliant blue sky.

"God's creation is something to behold isn't it, Mac?"

Outwardly, Mac Walker gave a brief smile, while inwardly he was shaking his head. The subject of God was one he wished to avoid. He'd seen enough blood in his still relatively young life to come to the conclusion there was no higher power, or if some kind of god did exist, he, she, or it, could give a shit about humankind.

Suddenly, the 767 felt as if it plunged downward then shook violently for several seconds, before resuming its more gentle upward motion. Mac noted the seatbelt sign remained on. Normally once a plane neared twenty thousand feet or so, the sign was turned off.

Mac Walker watched as the air marshal called over one of the two female flight attendants, a tall, broad shouldered blonde in her early 30's. She leaned down as he whispered something into her ear and then quickly made her way toward the cockpit.

The aircraft once again shook itself like a soaked dog, causing several of the passengers to cry out softly, their tone a mixture of fear and humor. Mac looked over at Eldra and saw her sitting with her eyes closed and her mouth moving silently as she recited a prayer to herself.

"It's going to be fine, Eldra – just a little turbulence. It's very common, especially during the ascent."

Eldra opened her eyes and smiled warmly back at Mac, her right hand moving to rest once again on top of his left forearm.

"You fly often, Mr. Walker?"

Mac nodded.

"Yeah, more than I care to actually."

Eldra cocked her head slightly to the right, unsure if she should press with more questions, or let Mac be. She opted for more questions.

"If you don't mind my asking, what kind of business do you do, Mac?"

The none of your business, business, lady.

"I was in the military. Now...I'm weighing my options. This trip was meant as a little vacation before making a decision on what I should do next."

Eldra's eyes widened as she nodded a few times while looking up at Mac.

"Yes, you have that way about you and I say that as a compliment. My Howard served in Korea, God rest his soul, heart attack four years ago. He was a Marine over there, gave him the Bronze Star. Not sure why...Howard didn't like to talk about it."

I know the feeling.

The plane shook again, and then again, this time causing several more passengers to cry out. Mac looked ahead and locked eyes with the air marshal, who was staring back at him with an oddly intense glare. He then rose from his seat and walked quickly past Mac on his way to the back of the plane.

Maybe he's gonna be sick.

Mac Walker's instincts informed him it wasn't sickness the air marshal was dealing with, but something else.

"Oh, I thought we were supposed to stay in our seats. Why is that man walking around the plane?"

Mac ignored Eldra's question as he conducted another quick survey of his immediate surroundings. Silent, growing fear was the prevailing emotion on the faces of those around him. That was to be expected given the amount of turbulence. What wasn't normal was the strain on the face of another female flight attendant who at that moment, emerged from the front of the plane, her eyes scanning the occupants before coming to rest on Mac Walker. She was of average height and build, likely a few years shy of forty, her light brown hair pulled back neatly from her head in a tightly wound bun. She had the somewhat flat, wide face of an Eastern European, possibly Russian. It was her eyes that really caught Mac's attention though – a flinty dark that continued to stare at him with barely concealed aggression.

The air marshal moved past Mac on his way back to his seat, nodding briefly to the flight attendant before sitting down. She continued to stare at Mac a moment longer before disappearing once again to the front of the aircraft.

What the hell is going on here?

Mac's unspoken question to himself would be answered soon enough.

2.

"I'm sorry, do you mind moving over? I just have to get away from the guy sitting next to me. He won't stop trying to flirt me up."

Mac Walker looked to his right and was greeted by an incredibly attractive woman of thirty or so years, with long, thick black hair that hung over her shoulders. Her large, deep blue eyes contrasted with the dark hair, and lent her face an air of uncommon elegance. A pair of full red lips was found under a just slightly longer than normal, Romanesque nose. Her fashionable and immaculate white blouse clung to a lean, yet quite feminine upper body that Mac found himself trying hard not to stare at. The first three buttons of the blouse were open, revealing the upper half of what were beautifully ample breasts.

Without thinking, Mac found himself moving into the empty seat next to him, his shoulders now just inches from touching Eldra who appeared fine with the newly arrived member of their shared aisle.

"Hello, young lady, my name is Eldra Peabody."

The younger woman flashed a brilliant white smile, exposing a row of perfectly proportioned teeth – the kind that were the result of considerable time and expense.

"Nice to meet you, Eldra, my name is Stasia Wellington."

The woman then looked directly into Mac's eyes as her mouth hinted at another smile.

"And who are you?"

Mac cleared his throat, glanced at Eldra for a second before looking back at Stasia.

"Name's Mac – Mac Walker."

Stasia extended a delicate, long fingered right hand which Mac then shook gently with his own far more calloused, battle roughened version.

"Very nice to meet you, Mac, you're my knight in shining armor."

Stasia's voice had a low, soft and soothing tone to it with a hint of an accent that was difficult to place. It was a breathy whisper Mac found instantly attractive. The kind of voice you wouldn't mind falling asleep to.

Once again the 767 trembled as it moved through another pocket of turbulence. The seatbelt light remained on, and Mac noted the mood of the plane's occupants understandably grew increasingly nervous.

"Ladies and gentlemen, the captain asks that you please remain in your seats and that there is to be no use of any electronic devices until further notice. Thank you."

Mac's attention to Stasia was momentarily diverted by the announcement. In all his time spent flying, he had never heard a turbulence related announcement quite like it. The tone bothered him as well. The female flight attendant's voice betrayed a nervous tension quite uncommon to in-flight announcements.

We're no longer ascending. In fact, it feels like we've been descending the last few minutes, but why?

Some forty minutes into the flight should have put the 767 over the area where the English Channel merged with the Atlantic Ocean and yet, Mac's interior compass told him they were nowhere near that normal Paris to Washington D.C. flight path. A quick look outside the window confirmed the plane was once again flying in the cloud cover though Mac knew they should have been well above it by now.

"Is everything ok, Mac?"

Stasia's question was left unanswered as Mac's eyes peered out through the window, trying to see any clue below as to their actual location. No such clue could be found though, rather only a thick swirling mass of seemingly impenetrable white.

"Oh my god!"

The words originated from a woman behind Mac, her scream ringing throughout the cabin as the 767 suddenly veered sharply to the left, the whine of its massive twin turbine engines causing the passengers' seats to gently vibrate with considerably more intensity than before.

"My goodness, this isn't normal is it?"

Mac looked down to see Eldra's right hand clawing at the rolled up sleeve of his open collared, light blue dress shirt.

"No, Eldra, it isn't, but don't worry these planes are built tough. Maybe they're just maneuvering past another bad patch of turbulence."

Even as Mac spoke the words of comfort to Eldra he didn't believe them, as an all too common phrase whispered inside of his head, words spoken to himself during countless conflicts as a Navy SEAL.

Shit ain't right.

Mac Walker's training and experience were quickly taking over. No longer was he merely a powerless passenger on a flight back from an all too brief Paris vacation. He was a trained killer, a man of action, and one who knew when taking control was not a matter of if, but when.

He wanted answers, and he wanted them now.

3.

"What are you doing? The captain said no electronic devices."

Mac ignored Stasia, focusing instead on powering up his cell phone. The battery was charged fully, but it was unable to establish a satellite connection.

"Mr. Walker, please don't do that. The captain said…"

Mac looked over at Stasia, noting how her words didn't indicate fear, but rather a superiority over him, as if she were in charge of his actions.

"I know what the captain said, but something about all of this isn't right. I need you to be quiet, Ms. Wellington. You're welcome to go back to your own seat if you want."

Stasia's face crumpled into itself just slightly, as if her feelings had been hurt.

"I didn't mean to try and tell you what to do, Mac. It's just the captain said…"

The woman's voice trailed off as Mac looked over at a young black man in his 20's sitting directly across the aisle from him. He wore the baggy street-inspired fashion so popular among his age group, including the all too common backwards baseball cap that sat to the side of his closely shaved head.

"Excuse me, can you see if your phone will get a signal?"

The man turned his head slowly to stare back at Mac, his eyes bloodshot and unfocused.

He's stoned out of his damn mind.

"Yeah, your phone, can you see if it gets a signal?"

The man sat motionless for several seconds before nodding his head slowly while grinning.

"No problem, man."

Mac watched as the man withdrew a cell phone from the right pocket of his dark grey sweatshirt and stared down at it. A half minute passed before he shook his head and shrugged, his eyes retreating once again into the drug induced haze that was likely his day-to-day existence.

"No go…got nothin'."

The 767 was vibrating even more violently than before, the roar of its engines drowning out any other sounds inside the cabin. It felt as if the plane was being pushed to its 570 miles per hour limit. Mac decided it was time to speak to a member of the flight crew to try and find out what was really going on. As he began to rise from his seat, Stasia's left hand clamped around his right forearm.

"What are you doing? You can't just get up. We're all supposed to remain in our seats."

Mac gently removed his arm from Stasia's grip and glanced toward the air marshal in front of him, and then turned his head to look to the back of the plane. There were no flight attendants to be found.

"You moved yourself to sit here, right? Don't worry, Stasia I'll be right back."

"Hey, asshole - sit down!"

The directive came from a goateed, heavy set man seated in the row behind Mac who had an American flag tattoo on one of his large forearms with the words *American Badass* scrawled over it. He was the father of the boy who had been kicking Mac's seat earlier, the same child who now sat silent and afraid as the 767 continued to shake all around them.

"You heard me, sit down. We ain't supposed to get up."

Inside his head, Mac Walker slowly counted to ten, trying to remain calm and not throat punch the buffoon, who had crossed his heavily tattooed and fleshy forearms across his broad, man-boobed chest.

Tattoos. I'm so damn tired of wanna-be toughs and their tattoos. Fat chunks like this asshole to pathetic girls with far too many insecurities and not nearly enough common sense.

"Don't make me tell you again buddy – SIT YOUR ASS DOWN."

Mac felt his right eye twitching, an uncontrollable tick that often revealed itself just prior to his dealing out some serious whoop-ass on someone.

"Please, Mac, just do what he says. We don't want any trouble. People are getting scared. I'm scared, and Eldra's probably scared too."

Stasia's soothing tone brought Mac back from the precipice of direct confrontation with the overly confident father seated behind him. He looked down at Eldra who offered a thin smile, her eyes confirming she was in fact afraid.

"Whoa! What the hell is that?"

It was the young black man who cried out the question as Mac felt the plane's entire structure cry out in protest as the floor beneath their feet literally buckled inward several inches, causing several more passengers to scream including the father who had just recently warned Mac to sit back down.

Mac looked around and again found no sign of any flight attendants trying to calm the passengers. He also noted the air marshal's seat was now empty as well.

And not a word from the captain.

Another powerful shudder shook the 767 as the floor buckled once more. Mac closed his eyes as he sat back down in his seat, trying to focus his thoughts on what might be happening. The only thing he could think of that might cause the kind of strain coming from the bottom half of the plane would be if its cargo door had been opened while in flight. He recalled a drop in mission during his time with SEAL Team Six, when he and nine others jumped from the open cargo door of a C17 as it flew over the rolling hills of Liberia. The C17 had made a similar shudder as its cargo door opened, though being built for such use, didn't feel like it was about to break apart as did the 767.

Why would they be opening the cargo door of a passenger jet while it's still in the air? That would be suicide.

"Oh my goodness, we're almost touching the water!"

Mac opened his eyes to look out the window next to Eldra and was shocked to find she was right, the 767 was no more than a few hundred yards above what must have been the Atlantic Ocean.

The plane's engines were howling with even more intensity as the 767 pushed upward away from the water and back into the cloud cover. The g-forces created by the jet's ascent were enough to push every passenger firmly back into their seats, making it almost impossible to move.

Mac could see the mouths of the passengers open, though their screams were drowned out by the ear shattering din of the 767's twin turbine engines being pushed well beyond their intended capabilities.

Nearly a minute passed before the passenger jet emerged from the clouds and into the brilliant blue of a much higher altitude, and yet, the 767 continued to climb as the sound of the great machine's multitude of metal parts screeched under the strain of the ascent, the sound merging with the horrifying howl of the engines.

We're all gonna die…

4.

The former Navy SEAL couldn't help but chuckle at the thought of dying while a passenger on a commercial flight back from Paris. Of all the things he had seen and done, the bullets, blood, and chaos of a life so often lived with a finger on the trigger, death by vacation seemed preposterous to him.

Guess that settles it then – I ain't dying.

Mac attempted to rise from his seat but found his body felt as if a great weight now pushed him back down. He looked around and saw other passengers' heads dropping down onto their chests, while others were trying to move as he was, but instead merely floundering weakly in their seats.

To his left, Eldra's eyes were closed though her mouth was opening and closing as her hands slowly clawed the seat in front of her. On Mac's right the seat where Stasia should have been was now empty.

Mac leaned back into his seat, his mind trying to focus on where Stasia might have gone, though soon that focus dissipated as he instead began replaying his recent meeting with the Project Icon directors last week.

Project Icon was an off the books cooperative entity between high ranking members of Congress and the military, funded via a hidden Department of Defense slush fund and made up of operatives who had proven themselves capable of carrying out the most demanding and high risk military intelligence and operations assignments.

When Mac received a phone message from a man named Ray Tilley asking if he was interested in interviewing for Project Icon, Mac jumped at the opportunity. He was at the time languishing behind a desk inside the bowels of the National Security Agency at Fort Meade going over intelligence data and writing up scenario projections in a seemingly never ending process of replacing one pile of paper for another. For a youngish man who had just a few years earlier travelled the globe as a member of SEAL Team Six, it was torture.

Project Icon was Mac's ticket out of the office cubicle hell that was his existence at Fort Meade.

"Mr. Walker, can you please explain to us this description in your review file as being a soldier of great courage and dedication, who at times, displays an over-willingness to engage in conflict rather that consider alternative solutions?"

The two-star general who asked the question was a dime a dozen military pencil pusher. The general's eyes were a watery red, under which sat a pair of overly fleshy jowls. General Tinny was his name, and Mac disliked him the moment he stepped into the third floor Pentagon conference room.

Ray Tilley sat to the general's right. Tilley had been a longtime staffer for one of the highest ranking members of the U.S. military and worked as the direct liaison between Project Icon and those few members of Congress aware of its existence. Unlike General Tinny, Mac sensed Tilley was a good man who wanted the best both for Project Icon, and more importantly, those men and women responsible for carrying out its missions.

To the general's left was a middle aged, attractive woman by the name of Francesca Porter. She worked for the chair of the Senate Intelligence Committee. Ms. Porter sat silently watching Mac closely, also waiting for his response to the general's question.

"Well, General, I've always been one to believe the quickest way to the other side is by a straight line. When one is engaged in the act of saving lives, be it others or your own, pausing to consider alternative solutions is often a luxury one simply doesn't have time for."

General Tinny folded his smallish, soft hands on the conference table desk and leaned forward toward Mac.

"Well, Mr. Walker, would you say you're prone to looking for trouble, when the better tactic might be to try and avoid it altogether?"

Mac glanced at Ray Tilley whose eyes were pleading for Mac not to blow the interview. Tilley had carefully reviewed Mac's file, knew the extent of his experience and abilities, and very much wanted him to be a part of Project Icon.

"No, General, I don't go looking for trouble, but if it finds me I'm more than willing to kick the shit out of it."

Tilley winced at Mac's response while Francesca Porter's mouth hinted at a smile.

General Tinny appeared less than amused by Mac's bravado, his deeply lined brow furrowing as the corners of his mouth turned downward.

"This isn't a joke, Mr. Walker. Project Icon requires the very best of the very best."

Mac nodded his head as he stared into the general's glossy wet eyes.

"I assume that's why you called me in here for this interview, General. You want the best? Well here I am."

Francesca Porter stared at Mac for a moment longer before concluding the interview.

"We're done here. Thank you, Mr. Walker, we'll be in touch."

General Tinny appeared ready to say something more, but was cut off by Francesca.

"I said we're done here, General. I've heard enough for now."

Ray Tilley said nothing as he escorted Mac outside to one of the many Pentagon parking areas. Finally, nearly a hundred yards from the massive structure, he stopped.

"I have no idea if that went well or not, Mac. Tinny's an asshole, that's no secret around here. Maybe Porter liked you though and she has the ear of the Senate Intelligence Chair, and that could make the difference in your favor. Tell you what – how about you take a trip? You know, some time off? Your file indicates you haven't taken any vacation time in years so my treat – where'd you like to go?"

Tilley was right. Mac had been on the job in one form or another for a very long time. That was his nature. He was most happy when he felt he was being productive though he also thought perhaps a little down time wasn't such a bad idea though. Being a product of the American Bayou had always left him hoping to one day visit Paris and if Tilley was willing to foot the bill, all the better.

"I'm gonna take you up on that, Ray. I'd like to chill out for a week or so in Paris."

Ray Tilley didn't hesitate, his right hand clapping Mac on the shoulder.

"Great, I'll set it up for you. Can have a limo pick you up and take you to the airport first thing tomorrow morning. Enjoy yourself, rest, relax, and when you get back we should have word on whether or not you're gonna be a part of Project Icon. You know where I stand, Mac. You would be an incredible asset to the team. I've reviewed hundreds of personnel files, and very few of them indicated someone as talented and capable as you."

Mac's semi-conscious recollection of his initial Project Icon interview broke apart as the 767's passenger oxygen masks fell down from the plane's ceiling.

We've lost…pressurization. Altitude…too high.

Mac struggled to place the mask over his face and then turned to try and put Eldra's mask on her as well. His fingers wouldn't move properly though, and the mask slipped from his hands.

Not working. Not getting any air.

"This one is still awake!"

Mac heard the voice but it sounded as if it came from a great distance away, though he knew that was impossible. He was in the confines of a passenger plane. The source of the voice had to be very close.

It took every bit of remaining strength left in his oxygen depleted body for Mac Walker to will himself up from his seat as his eyes strained to focus just a few feet in front of him.

The blurred figure of someone, Mac couldn't tell if it was a man or woman, moved toward him. They appeared to be holding something up to their face but Mac's eyes were unable to focus more clearly to determine what it was, though his mind whispered the only logical explanation.

It's a portable oxygen mask. That means this thing was planned. My instincts were right...should have acted sooner.

"Sit your ass back down."

A pair of strong hands easily pushed Mac back into his seat. Any remaining strength in his body quickly dissipated as the lack of oxygen fully overtook him, and the world soon went dark.

5.

When Mac came to, he found his hands and feet secured by a pair of zip ties. Looking around, he saw every other passenger was bound the same way, including Eldra who sat motionless in her seat, her shallow breathing the only sign she remained alive. Stasia remained missing and there was no sign of the flight crew or the air marshal.

The 767's turbines were humming quietly now, no longer being pushed to their limits. Mac couldn't see outside anymore. All the plane's window covers had been pulled shut, preventing him from seeing if they were flying over land or water.

A dull, creeping pain covered him as his body slowly recovered from the earlier oxygen depletion.

They didn't kill us – at least not all of us. That means they need us for something. Now I just have to figure out what that something is.

Almost any other human being would have been overtaken by panic if faced with the same scenario as Mac Walker found himself in at that moment – a plane and its passengers clearly taken hostage, no more than six months after the terrible and tragic events of September 11th, 2001.

Mac Walker was unlike most though. He was a man who had devoted himself to the mission, whatever that mission might be, and this situation was for him, simply another opportunity to utilize those talents that had made him such a valued commodity for men like Ray Tilley and an organization like Project Icon.

The sound of footsteps came from behind Mac's seat, followed by a whispered conversation between the air marshal and one of the female flight attendants. Mac closed his eyes and remained still as he focused on what language the two were speaking to one another.

"They will be searching in the area of debris we left behind us. That will likely give us another twenty four hours. We're already two hundred miles from that location and in another two hours will be landing and safely hidden, so calm down because everything is going as planned. Even if they figure out our flight path, we will use the passengers as our shield. They won't risk killing us all. Not yet."

They're speaking Bosnian.

Between 1993 and 1994, Mac Walker spent nearly nine months moving throughout the region of the Bosnian War during the ethnic conflict that erupted between those small Eastern European nations following the collapse of the Soviet Union. It was a time of brutality between people the likes of which even a hardened Navy SEAL was not fully prepared to witness. Women and children were rounded up, raped, beaten, tortured, limbs cut off, decapitations, entire villages wiped out.

Bosnians were primarily a Muslim people surrounded by Christians. While the media often portrayed Bosnia as the victim, Mac Walker knew better. All sides in that conflict were more than capable of repeated and horrific acts against each other. As is so often the case in war, there were no clearly defined good and evil – but simply mayhem, suffering, and death.

What are Bosnians doing taking over a passenger flight from Paris to Washington D.C.? Are the pilots also involved, or being forced against their will to do so?

Mac watched with barely open eyes as the air marshal and the flight attendant moved past him toward the front of the plane, his mind going over the details revealed to him in that all too brief conversation.

The air marshal mentioned debris being left behind. That must have been when I felt the cargo door opening beneath us. The rescue deployment will be focusing on that area of debris. A rapid descent, a debris trail left out over the water, then they climbed to 40,000 feet or more and depressurized the cabin to incapacitate the passengers. Got us tied up, the windows closed, and heading to God knows where. He said they would be hidden in two hours, so this isn't a suicide mission. At least not at this point.

Mac couldn't help but smile as he contemplated what he had managed to get himself into.

Tilley sent me on this vacation to rest and relax. Thanks a lot, Tilley you asshole.

Eldra began to stir next to Mac, her eyes slowly opening and then looking around her in panic.

"Sshh...it's ok, Eldra. I need you to sit there as quietly as possible right now. You don't want to get their attention. The more they think we're incapacitated, the longer I have to try and figure out my next move."

The older woman looked at Mac and then nodded slowly, letting him know she understood. The former Navy SEAL admired how quickly Eldra adjusted to what was a remarkable and likely very dangerous situation.

Tough old girl knows when to follow orders. That leaves the rest of the passengers to worry about, including the prick sitting right behind me.

As if on cue, the heavy set goateed man let out a loud groan.

"What the hell…why am I tied up? What's going on? Hey! What is going on?"

Mac could feel the man struggling in his seat.

"Sir, I need you to calm down. We don't need them coming out here and hurting you or anyone else. Take care of your son, make sure he's ok."

"Don't tell me what I need to do! You calm down! You calm down!"

The man's voice was nearly screaming as his body catapulted itself forward, his shoulders mashing against both Mac and Eldra's seats.

"Young man, please do what he says! Calm down and see if your boy is ok."

The man continued to struggle, trying to lift himself from his seat despite his bound hands and feet.

Mac Walker's patience had run out. The man was certain to bring unwanted attention to them. He half stood up and turned around in his seat, his eyes locking with those of the increasingly panicked father.

"I told you to sit down and shut up."

The simmering tone of Mac's voice caused the man to hesitate, as he glared back at his fellow passenger. This hesitation quickly dissipated though as he lunged forward, his mouth twisted into a snarl.

"I'd like to see you try and make me asshole!"

Mac clenched his teeth and sent his forehead crashing into the space just above the man's nose. The precisely powerful head-butt delivered the result Mac intended, causing the other man to crumple back into his seat where he remained unmoving, once again unconscious.

"Damn, you kill him?"

Mac turned his head to look at the young black man seated across the aisle from him.

"No, he'll be fine."

The younger man's eyes were wide as he looked Mac up and down, wondering what kind of man was able to incapacitate another man so easily.

"You some kind of soldier?"

Mac Walker leaned down to look at the father's young boy, who sat quietly breathing in his seat, not yet having woken up. Mac was glad the child didn't see his father taken down by him. Even if his dad was a world class asshole, a boy needed a father to believe in, not one to despise or think less of.

"I said, you some kind of soldier, man?"

Mac grunted as he sat back down in his seat.

"Yeah...I'm some kind of soldier."

6.

Over the course of the next ten minutes, more and more passengers began to stir. Their faces were masks of confusion and fear as they tried to determine what was going on.

"Everyone – your attention up here! Everyone! Look here!"

The air marshal stood with his feet spread shoulder width apart glaring back at the passengers. His eyes gleamed with determined excitement, the lower lip of his mouth curling downward under the large mustache.

A woman near the front of the plane began to cry, resulting in the air marshal quickly moving to her seat and smacking her across the face with the back of his hand. Mac could hear the boy behind him begin to cry as well as the sound of the slap reverberated inside the confines of the cabin.

"Son, listen to me. Your father is right next to you, and he'll be waking up soon. I need you to sit there and be as quiet as possible, ok? Be a good boy, and try not to make a sound."

The child's whimpering subsided.

The air marshal returned to his position at the front of the plane, his left hand pointing to the woman he had just hit.

"See? That is what you get if you don't pay attention! There will be no shouting, no crying out, just you sitting in your seats waiting for my instructions. If you don't do that, then you will be punished. Maybe the person next to you will be punished. Women, children, it doesn't matter. So nobody messes up, ok?"

To emphasize his point, the air marshal withdrew his handgun and held it in his right hand, pointing it at various passengers who sat in fearful silence.

"I will kill you if I have to. Don't test me. Just stay in your seats and keep quiet."

"We might all feel a little more calm if you take a moment to tell us why you're doing this."

Mac's statement filled the space between himself and the air marshal where it remained unanswered for several seconds.

"I didn't ask for any questions."

Mac Walker adjusted his body in his seat so that he was leaning to the right, allowing him an unobstructed view of the marshal. Their eyes locked as Mac held his stare until it was the air marshal who finally looked away.

"I don't mean any disrespect. It's just that you'll probably find us a lot more cooperative if we know what's going on – why you're doing this."

The air marshal's eyes filled with rage as he walked toward Mac's seat with his gun held in front of him.

"You want to be a hero, army boy? Yeah, I heard you talking to the old lady. Told her you were former military. Well guess what, I'm former military too, and unless you shut your goddamn mouth I'm gonna be killing some of these passengers. Their deaths will be your fault, understand? Maybe I start with that kid sitting behind you."

The air marshal stood directly over Mac, his mouth curled into an animalistic snarl as trickles of sweat marked the sides of his face.

"No, that won't be necessary. I was just trying to help you calm everyone down."

The butt of the handgun crashed into Mac's forehead, snapping his head back and nearly knocking him unconscious.

Ouch – that's gonna leave a mark.

It took a moment for Mac's vision to clear, allowing him to stare back up at the air marshal.

"You need another one, army boy?"

Mac shook his head, wincing as the pain from the blow to his head reverberated throughout his upper body.

The air marshal leaned down triumphantly, his sour breath scorching across Mac's face.

"That's what I thought. No time to play hero today."

Mac lifted his hands up slightly onto his lap and spread his wrists slightly apart inside the confines of the zip tie. He made it appear as if he didn't want the air marshal to see him doing so, when in fact, being seen was exactly what he hoped for.

"Oh no, there'll be none of that."

The air marshal reached down and pulled, causing the zip tie to cut into the flesh of Mac's wrists.

"There, that's better."

Mac watched as the air marshal returned to his position at the front of the plane, the man's face betraying his over-confidence in believing he had successfully intimidated the only passenger who might present a threat to his authority.

"If everyone cooperates, we'll be touching down soon. You'll be allowed to leave the plane, and go on with your lives, ok? But if you don't follow my orders, then there's gonna be trouble. People will be hurt or killed. Anyone here not understand what I'm saying?"

The passengers remained silent as the soft hum of the 767's turbines indicated to Mac they were travelling at a normal cruising speed of just over five hundred miles per hour.

"How about you, army boy, do we understand each other?"

Mac nodded once, though the faint hint of a smile communicated his certainty there remained some unfinished business between them.

The air marshal noted the smile, and appeared ready to make his way back to Mac's seat when suddenly the plane veered sharply to the left and then began descending rapidly, causing several of the passengers to scream out.

Mac Walker ignored the panicked cries of the passengers, instead focusing his full attention on the air marshal who had turned to run back toward the front of the 767, his gun still drawn.

Whatever that just was, he didn't expect it. That tells me something is going on in the cockpit of this plane.

The plane continued to fall from the sky, the hard left turn increasing as the chorus of passenger screams intensified.

Mac closed his eyes and relaxed his upper body, grateful in the pain of the just tightened zip ties pressing into the skin of his wrists. Years ago during the initial phases of his DEVGRU training, he had watched as a twenty-year Navy SEAL veteran demonstrated how one needed no more than a second, and a moderate tolerance for pain, to effectively escape from a zip tie binding.

The grizzled SEAL was a short man, no more than five six, with a gaunt, deeply lined face, and eyes that seemed barely to move while at the same time taking in every detail of his surroundings.

"The tighter the zip tie around your wrists, the easier the escape. Relax your body, take a deep breath, raise your arms, and then simply roll your shoulders forward as you slam the wrists down onto your midsection."

Mac and his fellow recruits watched as the longtime SEAL snapped the zip ties apart several times before instructing them to partner up and demonstrate they could do the same. Mac proved particularly adept at the maneuver, volunteering to break out of two and then three zip ties at the same time. By the end of the demonstration, his already considerable confidence was fortified even more by the newly acquired knowledge.

That was, until the SEAL instructor stood next to Mac and then secured Mac's hands behind his back.

"Ok, son, show me what you got."

Mac Walker didn't hesitate, simply mirroring the same motion, but doing it from behind his body. His arms rose up, and then slammed down into the backs of his thighs, once again breaking the zip ties.

The veteran SEAL's eyebrows rose slightly and then he simply nodded, a sign of being impressed which Mac knew to be extremely high praise for any DEVGRU recruit.

"Good."

Mac now sat in the seat of a hijacked 767 and prepared himself to repeat that maneuver learned as a young recruit. His arms rose above his head, and then were brought down against his abdomen as he rolled his shoulders inward to create even more leverage against the bonds.

The zip tie broke apart just as they had done during his DEVGRU training. His hands were free.

His feet remained bound, but whoever had tied him and the others up, had made the mistake of doing so while leaving their shoes on. That made escape much simpler.

Mac merely placed his left toe behind the heel of his right foot and removed the shoe. Once that was done, enough space had been created to allow him to squirm his feet free from the zip tie. The former Navy SEAL then shoved his right foot back into its shoe and leaned across Eldra's just then waking body and slammed the window cover upward, allowing him to once again look outside the plane.

What the hell?

Below them and growing closer as the 767 continued its rapid and violent descent, was a vast mountain range looming just below them It seemed the plane's wings were nearly grazing the snow capped peaks.

Mac's mind reviewed where a mountain range of that size could be located given their initial flight path over water, the hard left turn, and now descent, and concluded it was most likely the Pyrenees Mountains of northern Spain, the natural and imposing barrier between France and Spain.

So we would be heading toward the Mediterranean – but why?

Mac had no time to answer his own question as an unmistakable sound echoed from the cockpit of the plan, the kind of sound a man such as Mac Walker was all too familiar with.

Gunfire.

7.

The screams of the passengers once again filled the cabin. Mac ignored them, his eyes locked on the front of the plane, waiting to see who was going to emerge from the cockpit area. The 767's flight stabilized almost immediately after the gunfire, slowly rising above the mountain range, indicating there had been a struggle, and that someone responsible for that struggle had been incapacitated, or more likely, was now dead.

"What did you see outside the window?"

The question came from the young black man across from Mac. His eyes were large round saucers in his head, as he glanced nervously to the front of the plane, and then back to Mac.

"C'mon man, what's going on out there? Where are we at?"

Mac had already closed the window cover and sat back in his seat, still staring ahead at the cockpit area.

"Nothing – don't know. We're headed somewhere, but I don't know where that somewhere is."

Mac decided the less other passengers knew, the safer they would be. He already had to deal with the passengers' collective fear over what might be happening to them. Full out panic would make the situation much worse, and greatly increase the chances of them all being killed.

"Was that a gun being fired? Did it come from the cockpit? Have they killed the captain?"

Eldra was the one to ask the question, having just awoken next to Mac. Though clearly frightened, Mac was again impressed by how calm she remained.

"Yeah, that was definitely gunfire, but the plane's flight was corrected, so they still have somebody up there who knows how to fly this thing."

"Why are you lying to us? Maybe you're one of them! He's lying everyone! He opened the window and saw mountains out there! A bunch of snow! Isn't it obvious? The plane has been taken! It's another 9-11! We're all going to die! We're all going to die and this son-of-a-bitch probably knows why! He's in on it! It's another 9-11 and he's one of them!"

Mac turned to face the man who sat behind him, while also noting the father's panicked rant had caused his son to begin wailing loudly as well.

"Oh shut up! Shame on you! Look at your boy there! You're scaring him! This young man here might be our only hope of surviving this…whatever is going on here. So just be quiet!"

Finished with her admonition, Eldra continued to glare at the father of the young boy, her head shaking in disgust at the man's accusations against Mac.

"Is he right? Are we flying over mountains?"

The black man repeated his earlier question to Mac.

"Yeah, he's right. I'm looking at them right now. A bunch of mountains and a shit load of snow. Where the hell are we?"

Mac looked up to see the young man who had been making out with the woman he sat next to shortly after the flight had taken off, now leaning across his seat and staring out a window.

"Sir, I'd pull the cover back down over that window if I were you."

Mac's suggestion was ignored as the man continued to stare out the window even as his wife, or girlfriend, tugged on his shirt for him to sit back down in his seat.

"Hey, I think I see water! Off in the distance, I think---
"

The young man's sentence was cut off by the re-appearance of the air marshal.

"What are doing? Did I tell you to do that?"

Mac sensed the deadly tone of the air marshal's voice. His eyes were locked onto the passenger who had been looking out the window, his right hand slowly rising until the weapon pointed directly at the younger man's head.

"You all want to see things, huh? Ok, I'll show you. I'll show you what happens when you don't follow my orders. You – come here. Cover that damn window and kneel down in front of me."

The woman next to the man began crying as she wrapped her arms and bound hands around his shoulders while pleading to the air marshal.

"Please, he didn't mean anything. He just wanted to see where we were. Please don't hurt him."

The air marshal stood silently for several seconds as he looked down at the couple, seeming to contemplate what he should do next.

"Is he your husband?"

The woman shook her head.

"No, he's my fiancé. We're engaged. He just proposed to me in Paris. We were on vacation and he…"

The woman's reply broke down into a series of sobs as she continued to cling to her boyfriend who in turn, looked up silently at the air marshal, his mouth hanging slightly open as his own eyes welled up with oncoming tears.

The air marshal offered the couple a thin smile as he looked down upon them. Mac felt a cold shiver move through him as he realized the danger both the man and woman were now in.

He wants to kill them both. He doesn't have to, but he wants to…

Mac's intuition was quickly proven right as the air marshal placed his gun directly against the boyfriend's left temple and then with his left hand, pushed the young woman's head so her face mashed together with that of her fiancé.

"I had a wife once, not so long ago. She was raped over and over again by soldiers who wore the uniform of the United Nations. They called themselves peace keepers you know. But they brought no peace to her or our village. They only brought pain, humiliation, and finally, death. It was a war you Americans watched on television between stuffing your faces with fast food as your president stuffed himself into the mouth of a fat whore. A war started by Vatican's Satan. So now here we are, and fate will decide if your fiancé can save you – one bullet, two lovers."

The 767's passengers were frozen in horror, most still unable to fully comprehend what was happening to them. Even Mac was uncertain what, if anything he could do. The distance between himself and the air marshal was too great, and if he was shot and killed attempting to save the couple, the rest of the passengers had little hope of walking out of this plane alive. Mac Walker intended to act, but the time to do so was not yet right.

The young woman, realizing what the air marshal was planning, attempted to pull her head away but it was too late.

The bullet tore through the left side of her fiancé's skull, ripping through his brain, striking against the bone of the lower right skull, and then lodging deep in the man's neck. The air marshal had released his grip on the woman's head, allowing her body to recoil backward as her fiancé tumbled forward, blood pouring from his ears, nose, mouth, and eyes as his heart continued to pump blood despite a third of his brain having been blown into oblivion.

The young would-be bride's mouth opened wide, but no scream issued forth. Instead, she remained like that in her seat, unmoving, her eyes vacant, staring into oblivion, the innocence of her former life forever altered by the twisted, emotional corruption of an air marshal gone mad.

That same air marshal stepped back slowly from the body of the man he had just murdered as his head slowly raised upward to allow him to look into the faces of the remaining passengers.

"Ok then, I will say this just one more time. Stay in your seats and wait for further instructions. If I have to remind just one of you of the rules again, many more will die."

"Uh, hey, you should know that the guy in front of me, he opened up a window and looked outside too. I don't want his screwing up to get the rest of us killed."

Mr. *American Badass* was giving Mac Walker up to a just-proven killer. Even Mac couldn't believe what he heard being spoken a few feet behind him. The black man across the aisle turned to stare at the man, his eyes indicating if he had his own gun, he'd likely kill him on the spot himself.

The air marshal made his way toward Mac, his gun pointing at the former Navy SEAL.

"Is that true? Were you looking outside too?"

Mac could feel the goateed father shifting in his seat behind him.

"I saw him do it. Just before you came back in here."

The young boy whispered a plea to his father.

"Dad, don't tell on the man."

The air marshal loomed over Mac, the cold barrel of the gun held firmly against Mac's forehead.

He wants me to try and disarm him, give him an excuse to kill more of us.

What the air marshal didn't know was that Mac Walker's hands and feet were no longer bound. Mac prepared himself to strike, confident his own lightning fast reflexes would in fact prove too much for the air marshal to overcome.

"Careful, he's not tied up anymore."

The air marshal's eyes widened as he took several quick steps backward while keeping his gun pointed at Mac.

"Hold up your hands, army boy - NOW."

Mac's unbound hands rose slowly above his head. The air marshal stared at Mac Walker through narrowed, increasingly suspicious eyes.

"Who the hell are you?"

For a brief moment, Mac's mind began replaying the infamous refrain of The Who's *Who Are You,* a favorite song from one of his favorite bands. In a life lived among the chaos of military operations both great and small, music had always been Mac's calming retreat, particularly when the difference between life and death was at its most precarious. So as he looked back into the eyes of the air marshal, and the business end of his gun, Mac Walker heard the defiant howl of Pete Townsend's guitar, the belligerent pounding of Keith Moon's drums, the ominous rumble of John Entwistle's bass, and the aggressive, growling snarl of Roger Daltry's voice.

"I'm the guy you don't want to mess with. But for now, you got the gun – your move asshole."

8.

The marshal stood staring back at Mac for several seconds, his eyes clearly communicating his desire to simply kill Mac and be done with it.

"Turn around."

Mac paused, contemplating his chances of rushing the air marshal and disarming him. The risk was too great. He would likely be shot, wounded, and possibly unable to then help the passengers with the other rogue members of the flight crew.

The air marshal smiled, sensing Mac was considering making a move.

"Yeah, go ahead."

As much as part of him wanted to do just that, the more rational and experienced part of Mac Walker knew now was not the time for action. He turned around.

The air marshal walked slowly behind Mac and then paused. Mac knew what was coming.

This is gonna hurt – again.

One well placed crack to the back of his skull with the butt of the air marshal's gun, and Mac's world once again went dark.

"Why you want to be a sailor, son? And talk straight – no bullshit."

After being knocked out, Mac's mind retreated to the memory of his initial recruitment into the U.S. military. The Navy recruiting officer's name was Lieutenant George Mackey, a tall, broad shouldered black man whose large brown eyes seemed to bore into Mac's soul, pushing past the layers of pretense and carefully constructed arrogance so common to young men still trying to figure out the world, and their place in it.

"I want to serve my country."

Lieutenant Mackey folded his arms across his large chest and stared back at the just turned twenty years old, Mac Walker.

"Son, I just told you not to bullshit me. Now you see, there's some recruiters, well, they'll take on just about anyone. I'm not that kind of recruiter though, understand? So I'm gonna ask you one more time, why do you want to be a sailor? And before you answer take a moment to really think about it before you open your mouth."

Mac's initial instinct was to spout off another cliché for wanting to join the military, but something in Lieutenant Mackey's eyes gave him pause. Mac didn't really know the man but he already wanted to prove himself to him, so he remained quiet as he gave genuine consideration to the question.

"The thing is, sir, I've always had a need to prove myself. I want to be challenged. It drove my momma crazy when I was a boy. Always getting scraped up, broken arm, cut open leg, it's just my nature. If there's a challenge, I want to face it. I've done a couple years of junior college since graduating high school, and I know that living my life through books, or sitting at some desk, ain't for me. I want to be out there actually *doing* the kinds of things a person reads about in books. I'm a good athlete, always handled myself well in a fight. It's not that I go looking for trouble, but I'll take it on if trouble comes looking for me, and do what's got to be done to kick its ass. So I figure maybe I have what it takes, you know? At least I'd like the opportunity to find out."

It was Lieutenant Mackey's turn to sit silently and consider Mac's words. Nearly a minute passed before his deep, Bayou-drenched voice followed up with another question.

"What scares you, Mr. Walker?"

Mac sat up in his chair and felt his mouth breaking into a small, knowing smile.

"I used to think nothing in this world scared me, sir, and I mean *nothin'*. Could be ten other guys wanting to do me harm, and I'd happily take 'em on and give as good as I got. My momma says I get that from my daddy. He's stern, don't tolerate foolishness, but for the most part is a quiet, solitary kind of man, but Mom says if he feels him or the ones he loves have been wronged, *watch out*. Something powerful, like some unquenchable righteous fire is in my daddy that will rise up and demand those who done that wrong be held accountable. Lately, as I sat in those junior college classrooms and looked out the windows watching the days turn to weeks and then the months turn to years, for the first time in my life I knew what it was to really be afraid."

The recruiting officer leaned forward, his arms now folded atop the small, metallic desk that was among the few pieces of furniture inside of the small, Dauphine Street Navy recruiting office in the heart of New Orleans. Lieutenant Mackey's face had softened as he nodded slowly back at the young Mac Walker, seeming to know exactly what the hopeful recruit was speaking of.

"Go on, tell me what scares you."

Mac's eyes wandered toward the street outside the recruiting office window, watching as the cars drove quickly by, reminding him of how one's own life seemed to pass by just as quickly as well.

"The thing that really scares me is living a life that ends without having any real meaning. I want to do something, and I think that starts right here right now in this office. Sir, you can help me to do something that has meaning. I want to see the world, and help others. I *do* love this country, and that's no bullshit. I love America, I love the freedom we have and I want to protect it for me, my family, and anyone else who feels the same."

Mac Walker grinned and then tilted his head toward the door.

"Besides, if I can't convince you to take me on, there's always the Army recruiting office down the road."

Lieutenant Mackey threw his head back and laughed before standing up and extending his right hand across the desk toward Mac.

"Welcome to the Navy, son."

As Mac took the recruiting officer's hand into his own, he found himself pulled forward toward Lieutenant Mackey, who again grew serious.

"I've always had a sense about people, Mr. Walker and I got a real sense about you. You *will* be living a life with meaning. I just hope to God there's enough people like you around when it's really needed."

Mac Walker didn't fully understand, or appreciate those words then, but that understanding would eventually come to him years later.

More than he could ever have imagined.

9.

Who's staring at me? What is this?

Mac Walker's mind was somewhat slow to recover from the blow to the back of his head, but a moment later he remembered his confrontation with the air marshal, the order to turn around, and now found himself bound to another body, crammed inside of one of the 767 bathroom stalls.

'Don't worry, I'm alive. They didn't tie you up to a dead person."

Mac's eyes slowly adjusted to the face directly in front of his own. It was the male flight attendant who had been staring at him earlier.

The flight attendant smiled, and attempted a shrug, though his arms were locked around Mac so tightly it made it difficult to do so.

"They used a bunch of duct tape. The air marshal said you were some kind of escape artist. Got us wrapped up pretty good here."

Mac shifted on his feet as he tried to tilt his head as far away as possible from the other man's face – a face he noted had a significant gash under the left eye and a deep bruise on the right cheek.

"My name's Walter, Walter Hill. I tried to fight them when I saw what was going on in the cargo hold. They were getting ready to open up the cargo door! Why would they do that? These people are crazy you know. I mean, obviously you know that already, right? I think they're planning to use the plane for something horrible. Like another 9-11 or something. I came out swinging but between the two other attendants, and then that air marshal with his gun, they knocked me out. I woke up inside of here, and then about an hour later, they brought you in and tied us up together. Now I'm thinking to myself, well Walter, you sure got yourself into a pickle this time, but at least the fella you're tied up to is a good looking hunk of a man!"

Oh God, just kill me now.

Walter, seemingly undeterred by Mac's attempt to push his face even further away from his, continued talking as if they were already the best of friends catching up on old times.

"Anyways, I don't know if it's the whole flight crew that's in on this thing, or just the other attendants and the air marshal, but I figure at least one of the pilots has to be with them too, right? I mean, they need someone to fly the plane. And did I hear gunfire out there? I wasn't sure, but it sounded like a gun went off, and I figured it had something to do with the air marshal, because believe me, I already know how he likes to go waving that thing all around. Then they brought you in here and I was worried they had shot you, but you seem to be fine, so---"

The pounding in Mac's head seemed to increase with every word spoken by Walter.

"Yes, a passenger was killed, a young man sitting a few rows up from me."

Walter tilted his head to the right as he mentally revisited where the passengers had been seated just before take-off.

"Oh, not the nice young couple, he's dead? They killed him? Why would they do something like that? My god this is awful! Why are these people doing this?"

Mac fought the urge to head-butt Walter into oblivion.

"Because that air marshal is a killer, and he wanted to make a point to the rest of the passengers. Keep them scared enough they won't put up a fight. It appears to be working – for now."

Walter began to open his mouth again but Mac cut him off.

"I need you to shut up, Walter so I can think."

Again Walter prepared to say something, and again Mac interrupted.

"No, Walter just nod that you understand you need to keep your mouth shut so I can assess the situation. Just nod your head Walter."

Walter nodded his head slowly.

"Good boy. Thank you."

As described by Walter, both he and Mac were bound together by several layers of duct tape. Each man's arms were tightly wrapped around the other, as well as the lower half of their legs. Getting out of this was going to prove much tougher than the zip ties, especially since it required the help of all too talkative Walter, a man Mac knew could very well be part of the 767's takeover.

Not impossible though. Just need some time.

"Walter, I need you to tell me everything you know about this flight crew. Have you worked with them before?"

Walter shook his head.

"No, this was my first time with them. I had just been assigned a new rotation by the airlines. I wanted to see Europe. I've been doing the New York to L.A. flights mostly for the last six years or so. Needed a change of scenery, but this wasn't what I signed up for. No offense to being tied up to you of course. You haven't told me your name by the way."

Mac shifted his weight to the right, trying to determine just how tight the duct tape binding was.

"Name's Mac – Mac Walker. Where you from, Walter?"

Mac could sense Walter's smile forming before it appeared.

"Are you interrogating me, Mac? Wondering if I'm one of them? Guess I can't blame you for that. I'd be doing the same thing if I were you. I mean, I was part of the flight crew after all."

"What about the captain or the co-captain, Walter? Have you flown with them before?"

Again Walter shook his head.

"No, this was literally my very first flight with them. I flew from New York to Paris with a different crew then transferred to this plane for the flight back from Paris to D.C. It's the same airline of course, but entirely different planes, different crew, and different captain. The two other attendants though, they seemed to know each other pretty well. They both have similar accents. Did you notice their accents? And now that I think about it, the captain and the air marshal sounded similar to them as well."

Mac's head snapped to the left, his face no more than a few inches from Walter's.

"You sure about that? The captain had an accent similar to the two female flight attendants?"

Walter nodded back at Mac.

"Absolutely – very similar."

"What about the co-pilot?"

Walter hesitated briefly before shaking his head.

"I don't think he said anything to me, just nodded when I introduced myself. He seemed very quiet, kind of bored, or maybe tired actually. I remember thinking he was probably doing a multiple flight schedule without any rest. The airlines really push the pilots sometimes. I've known them to go two days without sleep. They're not supposed to be doing that, it's against regulations, but they still do."

Mac stood quietly as he considered the information given to him by Walter, his mind creating options within options as to what might be happening.

"What about the captain? Did he look tired to you?"

Walter's eyes widened slightly, as if he was remembering something important for the first time.

"No, not at all. In fact, he seemed kind of amped up, you know? Like he'd just shot back a triple latte or something. And his eyes, he was really looking me up and down, but not in any kind of friendly way. More like he'd just as soon see me thrown off the plane. Or…or locked up in a bathroom."

Mac Walker managed a smile at Walter's attempt at humor, though his mind still suggested the possibility the man's seeming cool-under-crisis demeanor meant he was actually in on the hi-jacking, and was now engaged in trying to gleam exactly who Mac was, and how he came to be on this particular flight.

What about Stasia? What happened to her?

"There was a woman sitting behind me. Attractive, dark haired, said her name was Stasia. She had a slight accent as well, similar to the others."

Walter's brow furrowed as he tried to recall anyone fitting the description.

"No sorry, I don't remember anyone like that. Then again, I was kind of, well…*you* managed to catch my attention."

Mac did indeed recall the flight attendant walking past him while staring intently at his crotch.

"Yeah, I noticed."

Walter and Mac stood in silence for several seconds before Mac's voice spoke softly in Walter's left ear.

"I need to get out of this bathroom, Walter and that means I need your help to do it. So when you feel me start to move, I want you to move in the opposite direction, ok? And then I'll shift to the other side, and you do the same, but we have to keep it quiet. We don't want to get the attention of that air marshal or the other flight crew, understand?"

Walter's chin moved downward toward his chest as he grinned, his eyes staring into Mac's.

"Why, Mr. Walker it sounds like you're asking me to dance."

"If that's what you want to call it, Walter, fine, I don't give a shit. Just move in the opposite direction I am, like a tree blowing in the wind - side to side, side to side."

Mac shifted his weight to the left, and then to the right, pleased at how Walter shifted his own body perfectly in the opposite direction, while at the same time, Mac tried to ignore the feeling of their bodies rubbing against one another.

"You're a wonderful dancer, Mr. Walker."

"Walter…shut up."

10.

Mac and Walter pulled and slid against one another for nearly twenty minutes before Mac paused to see if any progress had been made in weakening the duct tape. The 767's engines continued to hum quietly beneath them, the plane now travelling at a leisurely pace to whatever destination the hijackers intended.

The tape weakened on the sides of each man's hip where most of the tension was being created. A little more time and effort, and Mac was certain he could break free.

As he and Walter continued what Walter preferred to call their "dance", Mac recalled a military operation two years ago twenty miles south of the Mexican border town of Ciudad Juarez. He and nine other SEAL Team Six members were transported under cover of darkness to a Sinaloa drug cartel compound that both Mexican and U.S. authorities believed was holding no fewer than twelve local and area government officials, including a just appointed police chief who had promised the day of being sworn into office to clean up corruption in the city of 1.5 million. He disappeared 24 hours later.

Mac's team entered the two-story white stone compound structure with no resistance. Just inside the main entrance to the building's great room were the bound bodies of nine people placed in a neat row on the brown tiled floor. Each body was decapitated, their hands and feet tied up with common duct tape. They had likely been dead for less than twelve hours.

The mission leader, a twelve year SEAL veteran and first generation American by way of Durango, Mexico, pointed down at the duct tape and shook his head with a mixture of sadness and disgust.

"All you got to do is twist that shit from side to side and it falls apart. Don't pull it, you just got to twist it. At least then you have a fighting chance and don't die like some hog tied up for slaughter."

With no lives to save, the mission was over. Mac and his fellow team members were flown out by helicopter back to the United States within the hour. Days later Mac was told by Martinez that their Mexican military counterparts were certain someone within the Ciudad Juarez Police Department had tipped off the cartel of the mission to save the hostages.

The missing police chief was never found.

Mac never forgot the instructions on how to escape from duct tape though, and now crammed into the cramped interior of a passenger jet bathroom, heard the words of Martinez echoing in his head once again.

All you got to do is twist that shit from side to side and it falls apart. Don't pull it, you just got to twist it.

Walter's forehead rubbed into the side of Mac's face, leaving a rather large layer of sweat in its wake. The flight attendant had begun to perspire heavily during their "dance".

"No need to soak me, Walter. Keep at it, and try and twist your body as much as possible when you're moving to the side, ok?"

Walter smiled, appearing to have forgotten all about the fact he and the other passengers were on a hijacked plane.

"Yes sir. You want some twisting? I'll give you some twisting."

Mac could feel the tape loosening just a bit more as Walter began grunting softly from his efforts. A few minutes later, and the area around Mac's right hip and wrist released just enough that the former Navy SEAL was able to pull his arm free.

Walter's eyes grew wide as his mouth opened, causing Mac a moment of panic that the other man would cry out.

"Keep quiet. We're a long ways from out of here."

Walter's mouth snapped shut as he glanced toward the lavatory door, wondering like Mac if someone was just outside keeping watch.

Mac began to slowly peel the layers of duct tape form their arms and legs, hoping the noise of the tape being removed was being drowned out by the sound of the 767's turbine engines.

It took nearly a minute to fully remove all of the tape. Mac pushed the remnants of tape into a pile inside of the sink and then backed away from Walter as much as the limited space of the bathroom would allow.

"No offense, Walter but I'm damn happy to not be dancing with you anymore."

Walter merely shrugged as his eyes lit up with the humor he still managed to find from the situation.

"None taken, Mr. Walker. I just hope it was as good for you as it was for me."

Mac Walker grunted as he shook his own head in response.

"Pretty sure it wasn't but thanks all the same."

Both Mac and Walter's eyes fell to the floor as the sensation of slowly falling passed through each of their bodies.

"We're descending again."

Mac knew Walter was right, though this time the descent was of a more common variety than the earlier falling out of the sky version that had sent the passengers into a panic.

"I need to get a look outside to see if I can tell where the hell they're taking us."

While reaching for the door Mac paused, remembering something Walter had told him earlier.

"You said you tried to fight them when you saw what was going on in the cargo hold – that they were trying to open the cargo door during the flight. Did you see anything else in there that was unusual?"

Walter's brow furrowed as he thought back to the encounter with the rogue members of the flight crew.

"No, I don't think so. Just that they had pushed a bunch of the luggage into a pile right next to the cargo door. I'm guessing so they could toss it from the plane. I asked them what they thought they were doing and that's when they jumped me."

Mac's mind began to formulate why the 767 was now descending, but not yet fully trusting Walter, kept it to himself. Instead he refocused on finding a way to get to a window so he could look outside.

Before he could begin to push the door open, Mac Walker looked down to realize someone was already slowly opening it from the other side.

Well ok then, here we go…

11.

Mac Walker stood as far to the side against the wall as the close quarter confines of the 767 lavatory would allow, while he gently pushed Walter to the other side of the tiny room. Mac's body tensed, ready to take on whoever was opening the door. As the door swung halfway open, Mac looked to see a pair of familiar, striking blue eyes.

Stasia's face peered into the bathroom as she looked at both Mac and Walter before glancing behind her.

"Hurry, follow me."

The whispered words were barely audible over the engine noise as Mac found himself as uncertain of Stasia as he was of Walter.

Yeah, but she knows I'm in here, so at this point, I have no choice. Play along, watch, and wait.

Mac followed Stasia out into the narrow 767 cabin hallway as she made her way as quietly as possible toward the very back of the plane. Walter trailed close behind Mac. The passengers remained in their seats unmoving, and Mac saw no sign of any of the other flight crew.

Stasia disappeared behind a dark blue curtain separating the main cabin from the in flight food prep area. Mac was surprised at how large the prep room was as Walter closed the curtain behind them.

"The others are at the front of the plane. I believe two are in the cockpit, and two others just outside the cockpit door in the First Class section."

Mac nodded once at Stasia as Walter opened the curtain a few inches to peek down the cabin hallway. It remained clear.

"Still no sign of anyone else, Mac."

Mac looked around the food prep room and then back to Stasia, his suspicious nature still on high alert.

"Where were you hiding? Or, maybe I should ask you how you knew to hide before anyone else did?"

Stasia reached down with her right hand and pulled back a stainless steel sliding door revealing a small pantry area that ran along the lower left half of the room's wall.

"That's where I hid after sitting next to you, Mr. Walker. Then I heard them taking someone into the bathroom, and I thought it might be you. I was watching you before take-off. You looked like someone who knew his way into or out of trouble."

Stasia then stood silently looking back up at Mac, as Walter's eyes glanced from one, and then the other.

"Are you avoiding telling me how you knew to hide in the first place?"

Mac's question made Stasia smile as her eyes remained locked on his.

"No, Mr. Walker, I'm just wondering if you're worthy of my trust."

It was Mac's turn to smile.

"Funny, I was thinking the same thing about you."

Both Mac and Stasia then turned their heads to stare at Walter, causing the flight attendant to step back, his face a mask of offended outrage. Walter pointed his finger at the two others as he hissed his response to their accusatory stares.

"I got my ass kicked trying to stop whatever these murdering assholes are up to! We need to stick together, ok? So stop looking at me like that!"

Mac looked upon Walter a moment longer before again directing his attention to Stasia.

"Who you with?"

Stasia's eyes narrowed as she shook her head.

"What do you mean, who am I with?"

Mac was growing impatient. They didn't have time to be playing spy vs. spy.

"I mean what I mean – who are you working for? You're obviously not just a civilian. Far too observant and calm during what is clearly a crisis situation. That means training, and that means you're likely working for someone. I'd like to know who it is."

Stasia glanced toward the curtain and then lowered her eyes, seeming to engage in an internal conversation with herself over how much she should share regarding her identity.

"Vatican Intelligence Service, Mr. Walker."

Mac couldn't help but look surprised. He wasn't aware the Vatican had special agents, though if her just spoken words were true, Stasia appeared to be just that.

"Ok, if that's true, then what are you doing on this plane?"

Stasia hinted at another smile as she lightly tapped Mac's chest.

"You first, Mr. Walker. Who are you with, and why are you here as well? I spotted you right off you know. Like I said, I was watching you very closely, how you were looking around the cabin, noting where each passenger sat, the movement of the flight crew. You strike me as someone who's been in more than a few situations that were likely far too physically and emotionally challenging for most. And now, here you are."

One of the passengers began coughing no more than ten feet from where Mac, Stasia, and Walter stood behind the curtain.

"I'm former military – nothing special. But I will be more than happy to do whatever it takes to get these people home safe, so if you're hoping to do that too, then I guess we're on the same team. Oh, and this is Walter by the way. He says he's not part of the hijacking, tried to stop them, and then was knocked out. I don't trust him yet, but so far he's seems ok, but he's a shitty dancer."

Walter looked ready to say something and then closed his mouth and simply nodded toward Stasia, his eyes betraying an increasing nervousness.

"Well, any suggestions on how we proceed Mac?"

Mac noted how Stasia addressed him by his first name. Whether or not that was a sign she now trusted him, he wasn't sure, but he liked it, while at the same time hoping he wouldn't end up having to kill her.

"Someone's coming – one of the flight attendants. She introduced herself to me as Danika."

Walter leaned back to allow Mac to look for himself and confirm what Walter had just reported. The taller, blonde flight attendant was already halfway down the cabin hallway, her face looking strained as her eyes avoided making any contact with the silent, zip tied passengers.

While Walter appeared near panic, both Mac and Stasia remained calm, waiting to see if the flight attendant intended to step into the food prep room. Stasia held up her right hand and put a finger to her lips while stepping to the left opposite both Mac and Walter.

The tall blonde named Danika stopped short of the food prep room though, instead walking directly to the same bathroom Mac and Walter had just escaped from. Before deciding what they should do to prevent the flight attendant from telling the others they had escaped, Stasia decided for them, moving silently from behind the curtain partition and sending her right hand slamming into the side of Danika's neck in a smoothly delivered judo-inspired, pressure point strike, a method Mac's own extensive military hand-to-hand combat training commonly referred to as, "knife hands".

Mac was familiar enough with the method to know he had just witnessed it being delivered as powerfully and precisely as he had ever hoped to do so himself – and by a woman no less.

The blow knocked the flight attendant unconscious as her body began to collapse to the floor, but she was caught with hardly a sound by Stasia, who began dragging the larger woman back behind the curtain.

Stasia looked up to see Mac staring back at her with a mixture of respect, attraction, and uncertainty. He still didn't know if she could be trusted.

"When she doesn't report back they'll be sending someone else, likely the armed air marshal."

Mac nodded back at Stasia. She was right, the flight attendant's absence would be noticed by the others soon.

Walter leaned down to try and feel a pulse.

"Is she dead?"

Stasia's mouth curled downward in disgust as she pushed Walter away from Danika's unconscious body.

"Of course not – I'm a professional. We need her alive so we can question her. She'll just wake up with a terrible headache, but otherwise, will be just fine."

Mac leaned down and found a pulse, and then nodded toward Stasia.

"I like your work."

Stasia's cheeks gave a momentary hint of a blush.

"Thank you, Mr. Walker, I'm looking forward to experiencing some of your work as well. I do enjoy someone who knows what they're doing."

12.

"Mr. Tilley, am I to understand that we have, or had, an operative on that missing flight out of Paris?"

Ray Tilley looked across the desk at General Tinny as they sat inside of the low lit conference room tucked away in a corner of the Pentagon's fourth floor, knowing Mac Walker had in fact been on the now apparently missing, Atlantis Flight 444.

"Mr. Walker isn't one of ours General – not yet."

The general's fleshy, well fed face fell upon itself into a look of abject disgust as he turned his head to the left to look at an immaculately dressed man by the name of Stephen Mardian who had considerable connections with nearly every high ranking politician in Washington D.C. Mardian's role was to oversee the continued funding of Project Icon, and at least in his own mind, was the unofficial head of the off the books organization.

Ray Tilley also considered him an arrogant, self serving pain in the ass. Both Mardian and General Tinny were made for each other.

"I believe the general is trying to express his concerns about any potential, perceived involvement our organization might have had in the plane's disappearance Mr. Tilley. Media speculation is running rampant, and it's as if the aircraft simply…disappeared. With public interest in the story rising, well, that means it becomes a political matter as much as a search and rescue operation. So what we want from you, are assurances that no connection will be made between Mr. Walker, and Project Icon."

It took considerable effort for Ray Tilley not to tell the other two men to go to hell. Tilley's primary concern was for the safety and well being of his operatives. Both the general and Mardian on the other hand, put continued funding and the furthering of their own careers and political influence as top priorities.

There was something in the general's look though to suggest the military bureaucrat's concerns regarding the missing plane went beyond Mac Walker's unrelated presence on that flight. The general, and likely Mardian too, was holding something back.

"I can assure both of you that there will be no link to Project Icon. Now if you don't mind, I'd like to hear the rest of this story. Why the meeting? Why the concern over a link to Project Icon? Even if Walker was already one of ours, which he's not, we're off the books. You both know that. So where is this concern really coming from?"

General Tinny leaned back in his chair and folded his hands in front of him, seeming to wait for Stephen Mardian to decide if any more information would be forthcoming. Mardian in turn sat silently ensconced in his perfectly tailored custom suit and tie, staring back at Tilley.

Quickly losing patience with the men's silence, Tilley rose from his seat and nodded to each of them.

"Ok, if you want to remain quiet and keep me out of whatever loop you two think you're in, fine. I've got things to do gentlemen."

"Sit down, Mr. Tilley."

The general's tone made it clear he wasn't asking.

Ray Tilley slowly lowered himself back into his chair and waited. General Tinny nodded once at Mardian, who in turn, slid a single, manila file folder across the table toward Tilley.

"Look over that and tell us what you think."

Ray looked at Mardian and then down at the folder before opening it. Inside was a simple intelligence brief on a very attractive woman by the name of Stasia Wellington, an apparent operative for the Vatican Intelligence Service. Her credentials indicated high intelligence, and combat qualifications that would rival those of any Ray Tilley had working for him within Project Icon.

"I wasn't aware the Vatican had military trained operatives of this kind."

Mardian's eyebrows rose slightly as he shook his head.

"They don't – not officially. Unofficially though, I'd put them right up there with the Israeli's Mossad."

Tilley, though impressed by the woman's credentials, was confused as to why he was given her file.

"And what does this have to do with Mac Walker, or the missing plane?"

General Tinny cleared his throat as he pointed toward the file that remained in Ray Tilley's hands.

"She was on that flight too, along with your Mr. Walker."

Tilley looked back down at the photograph that accompanied Stasia Wellington's file, wondering what a Vatican Intelligence operative was doing on a plane that inexplicably went missing less than an hour after take off. Perhaps it was merely another coincidence, similar to Mac Walker's own presence on the flight?

"I still don't understand what this has to do with Mr. Walker. Are you trying to imply he had some kind of connection to this woman, and/or the missing plane?"

General Tinny grunted as he pointed toward Stasia Wellington's file.

"The Vatican is asking us that very question, Mr. Tilley, so here we are now asking you. You're the one who brought us Mac Walker. You did the review of his file, you recruited him. And now...this. We have a 767 that's up and disappeared from the sky. No warning from the cockpit, no distress signal, and, just as the media is now reporting, *someone* in that plane turned off the transponder. The Vatican operative was on that plane for some reason, and now the Vatican is asking us why Walker was there as well."

Ray Tilley's eyes narrowed as he realized the implications of what General Tinny was asking.

"How in the hell did the Vatican find out about Walker so quickly? And why would they come to us just as quickly to ask about him?"

The general glanced at Mardian, who then quickly interjected.

"That information is not for you, Mr. Tilley. As you likely know, cooperation between various intelligence groups is a common and essential component to protecting ourselves from the bad guys. They had an operative on that flight. I will assume it has to be related somehow to why it has gone missing. They've already accessed the passenger manifest via Atlantis Airlines, initiated a review of each passenger, came across your Mr. Walker, and are now asking questions. Simple as that. The only thing somewhat remarkable in this scenario is how quickly they've gone about it. Apparently, we've all underestimated both the resources and capabilities of the Vatican's intelligence network."

"Ok, so what now?"

Tilley's question hung over the small conference room for a moment before Mardian provided a response.

"We've already reached an agreement with our Vatican counterparts and an administrative liaison for Atlantis. We intend to wipe any record of either Mr. Walker or this Stasia Wellington having been on that flight. The Vatican supports the decision and has already thanked us for our cooperation and continued discretion in this matter."

"What if the plane is still out there somewhere – and Mac Walker is still alive?"

Mardian shook his head at Tilley's proposed scenario.

"No, not likely, we've already received reports of a debris field about a hundred miles off the coast of France. French authorities hope to have rescue teams in the area within the hour. The initial review from the airline suggests a likely catastrophic failure of the plane's primary systems, including electrical. That plane, and everyone on board, are most likely several hundred feet underwater by now."

Tilley persisted, refusing to fully accept Mardian's dismissal of the possibility the plane somehow, somewhere, remained intact.

"But what if the plane isn't at the bottom of the ocean? What if it was hijacked and its occupants taken hostage? I have to assume the authorities are at least entertaining that possibility."

General Tinny cut in.

"Certainly, normal protocols are being followed by the appropriate agencies involved, but the fact is, we also live in a world where planes do unfortunately crash and people die. I'm with Mr. Mardian, that plane is gone, and so too is your Mr. Walker. Besides, even if by some unlikely miracle the plane, and Mac Walker, were still functional, do you really think he has it in him to take back an airplane from what would have to be a group of well trained hijackers, and then manage to return it, and everyone inside that plane, back safely onto the ground? No Mr. Tilley, that is almost as unlikely as that plane not having crashed into the ocean in the first place."

Ray Tilley stood up from his chair and glared back at General Tilley, his hands balling into fists at his sides.

"Did you even bother to go over Walker's file? Do you have any idea what that soldier is capable of? He's no military bureaucrat, General. Mac Walker has been out there in the muck and blood for years now, taking fire, and doing whatever this country has asked of him. What about the time he went back into hostile territory not once, but five times to go bring back the other men in his team who had become trapped behind enemy lines? *Five times,* General, Mac Walker risked his life while taking the lives of those who wanted so very badly to see him and his fellow soldiers dead. Twenty two kills in just over three hours, in some of the most brutal and dangerous conditions imaginable. After three hours, some forty heavily armed Lebanese militants ran from that one American soldier – Mac Walker. They thought he was a devil, a ghost come to take their souls. They were convinced he couldn't be killed.

"That's just one example of what Mac Walker is capable of General as you sit there on your ass, behind a desk, and ask me if it's possible for him to take back a hijacked airliner and return it safely?

"Hell yes it's possible. In fact, I'd go so far as to say if that plane was in fact hijacked, and Mac Walker is still alive among the passengers, those hijackers aren't long for this world. He'll find a way to kill every single one of them. If you are given an opportunity to ever see Mr. Walker again, General, I suggest you take a moment to really look him in the eyes. Then you'll know what I mean. There are certain people in this world you simply don't mess with.

"That's Mac Walker."

13.

"Look at me."

Mac was leaning over the flight attendant, who was coming to after being knocked out by Stasia a few minutes earlier. Walter had shown them an access door from the food prep area to the primary cargo hold, the same place he had told Mac he found the other members of the flight crew gathered shortly after take-off before they attacked him.

"Danika, I need you to look right at me and tell me what is going on with this plane. If you don't do that, there will be consequences for you, do you understand? Just nod your head if you understand."

Danika looked up into Mac Walker's eyes and nodded slowly, her lower lip trembling as she struggled to fight off tears.

"We weren't supposed to kill any passengers. They are to be dropped off, left there safely, and then the plane will be used to send the message, to punish the Vatican Satan. But…but those men wasn't supposed to be shot like that. Those poor, young men…"

Stasia leaned down next to Mac and placed a hand on each of Danika's shoulders.

"Are we going to the drop off location now Danika? Where the passengers are supposed to be left?"

Danika avoided looking at Stasia, instead keeping her eyes on Mac. She nodded her head again before beginning to sob.

Stasia continued, her grip on Danika's shoulders tightening.

"Where? Where is the drop off point?"

Danika shook her head, her eyes red, wild, near panic.

"I don't know! They didn't tell us, and we knew not to ask. We were just told there was an island where we would land, refuel, and the passengers and us would be left there, and the plane would fly off again to deliver the message to the Vatican. Nobody was supposed to be hurt except those who deserve to be."

Mac and Stasia glanced at one another before Mac gently removed Stasia's hands from Danika's shoulders and whispered to the trembling flight attendant.

"Who's in charge, Danika? Is it the air marshal?"

Danika's face twisted in disgust as a soft snort escaped between her sobs.

"Reyos? He's a pig. He killed the passenger, and the co-pilot. He's an animal. I don't know why Captain Rogers defers to him so much. I've never liked Reyos, never trusted him."

Mac was trying to keep tabs on the torrent of information spilling out from Danika.

Co-pilot dead – that would be the first gunshot we heard. She thinks the captain is in charge, but sounds to me like the air marshal is the one in control. He's the only one on the plane with a firearm. Some kind of mission to attack the Vatican? Use the plane as a weapon? Is that the "message" she keeps going on about?

"Were you sent to the back of the plane to check on Walter and Mr. Walker?"

Danika peered up at Stasia and then quickly looked back down as her hands opened and closed repeatedly while they rested over her thighs.

"Yes. Reyos ordered me to check on them. He said…he said the army boy needed to be killed. That I was to see if he was awake yet, and if you weren't, he planned to throw you out of the cargo hold while we were still flying."

Mac grunted to himself as he surveyed the cargo hold's interior. It was a narrow space, but nearly forty feet long, the metallic walls gleaming with an off white glow. Most of the passengers' luggage had already been thrown out shortly after take-off to create the deception of a floating debris field which allowed the 767 to speed away undetected as rescue efforts would be focused hundreds of miles from the plane's actual and always changing in-air location.

"Danika, did the pilot shut off the transponder? And earlier, I was unable to acquire a cell signal from the cabin. Is there some kind of electronic shield device being used on board?"

Danika shook her head as she closed her eyes tightly and inhaled deeply.

"I don't' know about any of that. Maybe…maybe Milla mentioned something about a signal being shut off. I don't understand those things."

"She's lying."

Stasia coolly hissed her condemnation of Danika's attempt to portray herself as a largely unknowing accomplice of the hijacking.

"She's a member of the flight crew. Walter, is it possible a flight attendant wouldn't know about the plane's communications system? A transponder?"

Walter was looking down at Danika as if she were some kind of pitiful creature incapable of anything other than being a sobbing mess.

"No, even I know something about those things, and I've never been one for the details. We get training on all of that, every year. I would agree with you – she's lying."

The floor beneath them began vibrating with quickly increasing intensity as an almost unbearably loud rumbling noise filled the confines of the cargo hold. Mac knew instantly what the sound was.

"They're lowering the landing gear!"

Both Mac and Stasia rightly assumed that meant the plane was nearing the drop off destination, the one Danika just told them she didn't know the location of.

"Where's the drop off location, Danika? And don't lie to me."

Danika's eyes filled with tears once again and she cried out.

"I told you, I don't------"

The cry was abruptly choked off as Stasia's right hand clamped around Danika's throat, causing the flight attendant's eyes to bulge and a barely audible gurgling noise to escape her open mouth.

"Look you little bitch, I don't have time to listen to you try and tell your friends where you are. And I sure as hell am in no mood to listen to you pretend that you don't know what's going on all around you. Mr. Walker here asked you a question. I suggest you answer him. Otherwise, I have no more use for you. So start talking. NOW."

Danika took several deep breaths as she massaged her throat with her right hand.

"It's somewhere off the coast of Northern Africa, an island. That's all I know – I promise!"

Danika stood back up and then reached her right arm out to brace herself as the plane began veering sharply as its descent continued.

"Your call Mr. Walker – what now?"

Mac looked up at Stasia and then back to Danika, before slowly standing up, his eyes peering toward the opposite end of the cargo hold where he saw the unmistakable outline of a door.

"Walter, where's the door down there open into?"

Walter took a step forward so he stood next to Mac as both of them now looked to the other end of the cargo bay.

"To the main boarding area. First Class is to the right, and the cockpit is just down the hall to the left."

Mac Walker decided a visit to the cockpit needed to happen sooner rather than later, but first, he had to deal with the armed air marshal, and that meant he needed some help from Danika.

14.

"Secure location seven - one hour."

Ray Tilley intended to call in a favor – a big one. He had left his meeting with General Tinny and Stephen Mardian knowing both men were holding back information regarding what might really be happening with that missing 767. The Vatican's alleged involvement added an entirely new dimension that Tilley was determined to find out more about. Even though he had just told the general that Mac Walker wasn't one of "theirs" yet, Tilley had been following Walker's military career for nearly three years, pouring over summary reports, intelligence data from across various agencies, and everything to date pointed to Mac Walker as having the potential to be Project Icon's best operational asset.

That made Walker worth protecting, even if he was stuck somewhere 40,000 feet in the sky.

Or he's already dead, like Tinny and Mardian want you to believe.

That was the rub. They *wanted* Tilley to believe Walker was dead so he wouldn't go chasing the alternative. Ray Tilley was rarely one to follow directives for the sake of directives. If he had an asset who needed help, it was his job to do everything he could to see that help was given.

Secure location seven was one of several places Tilley would sometimes meet with a longstanding NSA source who worked out of their Foggy Bottom apartment. Bradley Riker was a former college roommate of Tilley's. The two men had kept in touch over the years, and as Riker rose through the ranks at NSA, he and Tilley initiated on unofficial and ongoing quid quo pro arrangement where both men would provide information to the other. Tilley suspected Riker's primary means of obtaining intelligence data was from his own Communications Intelligence source who had access to the always accumulating Department of Defense materials. Tilley never asked who that source was, just as Riker never asked what Tilley needed the information for. Each man had long ago accepted that the less one talked about the specific obligations of their work, the better.

All that really mattered to Ray Tilley was that Bradley Riker was both very good at acquiring information, and even more importantly, could be trusted. Location seven was the corner of 19th and G. Riker was to wait on the sidewalk for Tilley's arrival in one of the multitude of black limos that were always crisscrossing D.C. Once inside the limo, the two men could speak without fear of being seen or heard, well hidden behind the vehicle's darkened privacy glass as the limo would simply continue driving until the conversation was ended, before dropping both men off at their chosen destinations.

Tilley looked through the privacy glass from the backseat of the limo and was pleased to see Riker waiting, right on time, as usual.

"Stop here, please, we're picking that gentleman up."

The limo driver, a balding, forty something man with unusually thick glasses, pulled the car over next to the curb, his eyes never looking to Tilley in the back seat. In Washington D.C., both limo and taxi drivers knew to avoid eye contact with the privacy seeking public figure politicians and politicos who were the source of their livelihood.

Just shut up and drive had long been the mantra for their line of work.

Bradley Riker appeared as Tilley had remembered him. Still lean, and an inch or two over six feet, with short cut dark hair that was just beginning to show the hints of grey at the sides. In college, Riker had always been the more successful with the girls, his easy going, confident manner and classic Ivy League good looks proving a capable combination that lured many a willing young woman to his bed.

Ray Tilley, though hardly a recluse, was more devoted to his studies, and far less confident with the opposite sex than Riker. As Tilley would be sitting alone in his room reading a book, Riker was oftentimes across the narrow hall of their rented two bedroom apartment, quite literally, pounding the flesh.

"Hello again, Ray. You're looking a little tired."

Tilley's face cracked the slightest of smiles as he waited for Riker to close the door.

"And you're looking like you still have the world by the tail, Brad. How's the family holding up?"

Tilley's greeting was no mere pleasantry, but rather a reminder of what Riker owed him. Five years ago, Bradley Riker's daughter Daniela had been hit by a driver who then sped off, leaving the six year old girl lying unconscious in the parking lot of their apartment complex next to what remained of the red tricycle she had been riding. Four months later, though the young girl had physically recovered from the trauma, she was left with permanent brain damage, and would never live a life without constant care.

The investigation by D.C. Metro seemed unwilling to pursue the whereabouts of the driver, and within two weeks of the hit and run, informed Riker the case was being filed as open, but no longer ongoing, with no active detective assigned to it. Bradley Riker spent the next six months consumed with finding who had struck, and then left, his little girl to die.

That search led him to a man by the name of Cylis Rohrs, who also happened to be a longtime senior staffer for one of the most powerful members of the U.S. Senate. That kind of connection would prove more than capable of squashing an investigation being conducted by D.C. Metro, perhaps the single most corrupt big city law enforcement agency in the nation.

Rohrs had long been known throughout D.C. as a boozer with an affection for call girls. One such call girl lived in the very same apartment complex as the Riker family. Her name was Tawnya and it took just a little cash and pressure from Bradley Riker to get her to admit that Cylis Rohrs had left her apartment drunk that same day and time that Riker's daughter had been run over. Tawnya also told Riker that Rohrs had not been back to her apartment since, but rather demanded she come to his place, which he had never had her do before.

After the call girl gave Riker Rohr's home address, he made the twenty minute drive across town to the affluent Dupont Circle neighborhood, where Cylis Rohr's rented a red bricked, tudor styled home at the end of a cul-de-sac of similar homes.

During that short drive, what little sense and reason that remained in Bradley Riker had left him. His only thought was revenge against the man who had brought so much pain and suffering to his daughter. He already knew Rohrs lived alone, having divorced his third wife over a year ago.

Riker parked across the street from the house and waited – a wait that lasted until nearly three in the morning. Finally, a large, blue, late model four door sedan careened into the driveway, its right tire running over the curb as the car lurched to stop in front of the two garage doors.

Rohrs stumbled out of the car and then fell to the ground, laughing to himself as he rolled onto his back. When the political adviser opened his eyes, he saw Bradley Riker staring back down at him.

"What is it? What do you want?"

Riker glared at Rohrs, noting the alcohol fed paunch, bloodshot eyes, and ample double chin that quivered as Rohrs attempted to lift himself off of the ground.

"You need to get off my property asshole, or you can help me up. Either one, take your pick."

Rohrs had half rolled onto his side, but then fell back down again. Riker was amazed the man had managed to drive his car this far given the extent of his inebriation.

Just like he was driving it the day he hit Daniela.

The reminder was too much, tearing apart the last vestiges of self control. Riker's right foot slammed into Rohrs' side, sending the older man gasping for breath as he scrambled across the driveway and toward the entrance to his home.

The second kick caused Rohrs to begin vomiting, the vast quantities of alcoholic liquid projecting from his mouth in a grotesque, cartoonish fashion as he continued to work his way toward the front door.

"You want money? I got it inside the house. Just don't kick me anymore, ok? Just...I got it inside the house."

Riker had grabbed Rohrs by the back of his collar and pulled, pushed, and dragged him to the front door.

"Open it."

Rohrs, whose reply came between a series of gasping gurgles, pointed toward the door handle.

"It's not locked. You can go right in, ok? Take whatever you want. There's not much."

That was when Riker saw the left corner of the car's bumper gleaming softly under the motion sensor driveway lamp. A small area of metallic red contrasted with the vehicle's dark blue, the very same red of Daniela's tricycle.

A pained sigh was the only sound Bradley Riker made before he grabbed onto Rohrs and shoved him into the front door.

"Get in there you drunken prick."

Rohrs opened the door with a trembling hand, his chest heaving as he struggled to catch his breath.

"Calm down buddy, just...take it easy, ok?"

Riker pushed Rohrs in the back after closing the front door behind him, sending the middle aged political adviser sprawling onto the hard wood hallway that led from the small foyer entrance.

Rohrs rolled onto his side, his panicked eyes looking back at Riker, already sensing this had something more to do than just a mere robbery.

"Please, whatever this is about, let's talk it over, ok? Let's just sit down and…talk it over."

The words were spoken in a whistling, wheezing type gasp as Rohrs continued to struggle for oxygen. Riker noted the man's skin had gone pale, and his face was covered in a heavy layer of sweat.

"You almost killed my little girl. Some days, when I look at what is left of her, I wish you did. Ran her over with your car and left her dying on the pavement. Hit her with the same car you have parked outside. Who'd you get to end the investigation? The senator you work for?   Some influential political donor? Doesn't matter, because it's just you and me now asshole. Just you and me…"

Rohrs looked like he was about to deny the allegation, but then seeing the rage burning within Bradley Riker's eyes, thought better of it. Instead he began sobbing as he sat on the hallway floor with his back leaning against the wall.

"I'm so sorry. I'm a sick man. I need help. I can't stop, I can't---"

Riker was in no mood for the pathetic bastard's bullshit.

"How about you just call a damn cab? You don't need to drive! Why do it? Why put so many other people in danger? Why run over a child, and then just drive off?"

The final words were shouted out by the NSA agent as his balled up right fist descended into the right side of Rohrs' face, the knuckled bone crunching into the political adviser's overly fleshy cheek. Again and again Riker struck the older man, for how long he couldn't later recall. All he knew is that each blow represented just a fragment of the pain Cylis Rohrs had inflicted upon the Riker family. Finally the punches stopped as Bradley Riker stepped away from Rohrs' battered and bleeding face.

The older man was barely moving, his breath now faint whisper, his eyes half open slits, glazed and unfocused.

Cylis Rohrs was already all but dead at that point, having suffered a massive heart attack that had begun shortly looking up at Bradley Riker looming over him outside his home.

Initially, Riker considered calling 911, but stopped when he realized he would most certainly be charged with Rohrs' death. It was Riker's NSA job which afforded them the kind of insurance coverage that provided Daniela the very best care. That care would go away if Riker were to end up in jail, leaving his wife and Daniela alone without the means to give his daughter the specialist treatment her condition required.

Call Ray Tilley. He'll know what to do.

Which is exactly what Riker did, closing in his eyes in gratitude when Tilley answered on the second ring. Riker explained the situation in thirty seconds, and then waited for Tilley's response, praying silently that his old college buddy wouldn't simply leave him on his own.

"Stay put, keep the lights turned off, and I'll be there in twenty minutes. Don't go outside. Don't do anything until I arrive. I'll be coming in from the back of the house, so make sure it's unlocked."

Tilley walked into the home through the back door in seventeen minutes. He said nothing as he looked around first at the body of the by then dead, Cylis Rohrs, and then the rest of the home, before finally addressing Riker.

"Your car is across the street, right?"

Riker nodded once.

"Good, I want you to go out the back, make your way to your car avoiding the street lights, and then drive home. Go straight home, understand? No stops. Go home, and then start work tomorrow just like you would any other day. Tell nobody about what happened here tonight, not even your wife. That hand there, you need to clean it up and then wrap it so it's covered up, and tell anyone who might ask, that you fell down and sprained it. Don't change that story. Just repeat it to whoever asks you. So leave here, go home, and I'll handle the rest. As far as you're concerned, this – whatever this was, it never happened, understand?"

Again Riker nodded just once, and then walked out the back of the home as Tilley had instructed him to.

Two days later he read the headline and brief accompanying story in one of the local D.C. newspapers regarding the death of Cylis Rohrs.

Cylis Rohrs, 59, was found dead in his home late yesterday morning by D.C. Metro police, the victim of an apparent car jacking and subsequent heart attack. The initial investigation, according to Metro P.D. spokeswoman Leah Brown, indicates Mr. Rohrs was left in an unknown location following the carjacking, walked back to his residence where he then collapsed inside his home. He had apparently been in poor health for some time.

Rorhs was a well known fixture among political circles in Washington D.C., having spent the last fourteen years as a senior consultant for Minnesota Senator Delvin Briggs.

Senator Briggs's office issued a statement calling Cylis Rohrs a "wonderful friend and great asset to our staff. He will be missed."

It was nearly a month after that announcement when Bradley Riker received a noon phone call from Ray Tilley, asking to meet him in the park two blocks down from Riker's apartment.

It was in the park, surrounded by various people jogging, reading, and walking their dogs, where Tilley indicated he expected the work performed on Riker's behalf regarding Cylis Rohrs be paid back at a time of Tilley's choosing.
"Some day I'll call in the favor, Bradley, and I need to know you can be trusted to pay up when that time comes."

Riker glanced toward an attractive woman as she jogged past where he and Tilley were standing, and then shrugged.

"Sure, you can count on me, Ray, no problem."

Ray Tilley held Riker's gaze for a moment and then shook his head.

"I'm not talking about a quick data reference Bradley, or a file that I can eventually get to myself. When I call in the favor, it's gonna be something big, something that puts your career, possibly even your life, at risk."

This caused Riker to pause as he wondered what Tilley might be involved in. He knew it was military related, though whatever it was, not even Riker's NSA clearances could pull it up, meaning it was totally off the books.

"You can trust me, Ray, but I need to know one thing."

Ray Tilley's eyebrows rose slightly as he stood with both hands stuffed into his coat pockets.

"What's that?"

"Are you one of the good guys?"

It was actually a question Tilley had often asked of himself. He looked out at the surrounding park, and the people who were able to carry on in considerable security having been blessed to live in a country where such security was an expectation rarely interfered with because of men like him, who worked to make it so.

"Yeah, Bradley, I'm one of the good guys."

15.

"Danika, I need you to look at me and listen very carefully to what I tell you, ok?"

Mac Walker knew the flight attendant was near her breaking point. He also knew that if they were to have a chance to get out of this alive, she would play an integral part in helping to make that happen.

"You're going to go back out there and act as if nothing is wrong. You tell the air marshal you checked on Walter and me in the bathroom, and we're tied up and secure, just like he left us, right?"

Danika's confused expression caused Stasia to curse under her breath.

"You can't be serious, Mr. Walker. You trust her?"

Mac leaned back and stared at Danika for a moment and then nodded his head.

"Yeah, and besides, we don't have much of a choice. She may be part of this mess, but I think she's having second thoughts. Maybe she's worried she'll never see her own family or friends alive again. Am I right Danika?"

Danika's eyes welled up once again with tears as she fought to look at least partly composed under the stress of the situation she unwisely had placed herself in.

"I can help you. I *will* help you. I don't want anyone else getting hurt. The passengers, I was told they wouldn't be harmed. It wasn't supposed to happen like this."

Mac nodded his head, appearing to Danika every bit the comforting, reasonable counterpart to Stasia's simmering rage and distrust.

"Very good, Danika. So walk out there and do what I said, and when the time comes, help us to help keep the passengers safe. Can I trust you to do that for me?"

Danika nodded as Mac helped her back to her feet while the tone of the 767's engines lowered considerably as the plane prepared to land.

With Danika gone from the cargo area, both Stasia and Walter stood staring at Mac in disbelief.

"What? I need to get into the cockpit, and to do that, we need more time to prepare. She'll buy us that time."

Stasia rolled her eyes and pointed at the door from which Danika had just departed.

"Or she sends that air marshal in here shooting."

Mac Walker merely shrugged.

"Then I deal with that if I have to. Otherwise, we wait for our moment and take it when it presents itself."

"Mr. Walker, I don't take unnecessary risk."

The former Navy SEAL grinned as he leaned down to whisper into Stasia's left ear.

"After you and me are done saving the world, we'll see about that."

Walter moved himself against the wall of the cargo hold and motioned for the others to do the same.

"Better hold on – we're about to land."

True to Walter's warning the 767's landing gear cried out several times as the wheels made contact with the ground, the force of the landing almost succeeding in knocking Mac, Stasia, and Walter off of their feet.

While Mac and the others were bouncing around the cargo area, the cockpit of the 767 was home to two very determined men. Reyos Huskich, the armed air marshal, was occupying the seat of the recently killed co-pilot, whose body had been crammed into the back right corner of the cramped space.

Flight 444's captain was a nearly twenty year commercial pilot veteran by the name of David Rogers. The name he had been born with though, was David Kurjak, the son of a Bosnian family who had been slain during the 1990's conflict that tore through his homeland. Kurjak had long left Bosnia by the time his family was murdered, having attended university in London, then moving to the United States to pursue a career in flying.

The war changed him though, just as he changed his surname from Kurjak to the more Americanized Rogers in 1996. It was then the seeds of his plan were initially planted, the desire for revenge having completely consumed his being until that revenge was the only thing left to him. David Kurjak watched and waited, and eventually found others who believed as he did, that the tens of thousands who suffered during the bloodshed and rampant inhumanities of the Bosnian Conflict must be made to pay for their sins, and there was no greater devil than the corruption housed within the confines of Satan's Church – the Vatican.

Allah demanded it so.

"Everything looks to be in order. It appears our Tunisian contacts have followed through with their promises."

Captain Kurjak glanced at the air marshal, and then nodded approvingly while expertly bringing the 767 to a stop on the narrow, compacted dirt air strip before turning its nose toward a large, metallic hanger with a green painted roof that made the structure more difficult to be spotted by overhead satellites.

"I told you they could be trusted. They feel as we do, all of us disciples of Torgal Al-Muhamed. So it was written, and so it will be done."

Reyos Huskich watched from the co-pilot's chair while a group of armed men emerged from the darkness of the nearby hangar as a thin smile crept out from underneath his considerable mustache, and then repeated the words of Captain Kurjak.

"So it was written, and so it will be done. All praise to Allah."

16.

"I need everything you can come up with on the missing plane out of Paris – Atlantis Flight 444. Any names, back stories, connections that seem odd, out of place, and pay particular attention to the flight crew.

"I also need you to run a full report on a Stasia Wellington. I'm told she's connected to Vatican Intelligence. I already know the basic information, so I'm counting on you to dig deeper, understand? Get me what they don't want me to know."

Riker looked at Tilley as the two men sat in the limo's backseat while the vehicle made its way slowly amidst the mid day D.C. traffic.

"Was she on the plane - Stasia Wellington?"

Tilley nodded while watching a motorcycle rider speed past them, weaving between cars on its way to some apparently urgent destination.

"I was told she was. I'm hoping you can confirm it."

Tilley sensed Riker becoming increasingly interested in the task. The missing plane had dominated the news that morning.

"Do you think the plane didn't actually crash in the ocean, despite the debris field that's being reported?"

Ray Tilley wasn't immediately certain how to respond, so finally, he decided to simply respond with the truth.

"I think that plane was hijacked. I think it's out there right now, somewhere, and whoever took it, doesn't intend to just give it back. The people I deal with aren't willing to disclose what they know, at least not to me. So, that's where you come in Bradley. I need you to tell me what they won't. Even better would be for you to give me information they don't yet know."

Riker looked ahead toward the limo driver, wanting to confirm the glass partition that separated the back of the limo from the front, remained closed, before whispering his next question to Tilley.

"I do this, and we're square, right? This is the big favor you said you'd be calling in after…"

Riker's voice trailed off, not wanting to actually speak directly of the Cylis Rohrs incident.

Tilley's mouth widened slightly into a thin smile as he nodded.

"Yeah, I'll consider the debt paid, but I need this fast, within the next few hours."

Riker's eyes widened as his mouth dropped open, shocked at the abbreviated time frame Tilley wanted him to work under.

"Ray, that's impossible! I have to work around protocols, hide my tracks, maybe call in my own favors to a few other---"

Tilley cut him off.

"You *can* do it, Bradley. Don't give me excuses, give me information. That's how this works. You do this, and you don't owe me for what I did for you."

Riker persisted in his belief what Tilley was asking of him was impossible.

"It's not enough time. I'll be caught, and then what good will that be for you and any future information you'd like to have access to?"

Ray Tilley had enough of Riker's hesitation, and turned to face him, jabbing a finger sharply into the other man's chest.

"Don't lecture me on worries about getting caught, Bradley. I could have got caught when I took care of that Rohrs mess for you. Yeah, I know you don't like to hear his name, but it happened, ok? You got scared, I came in and took care of all of it for you, didn't I? I did it because I consider you a friend, and I know that guy was the one who hurt your family. And then you gave me your word that when I asked for a favor, you'd agree to do it. So here we are, and you can either be a man of your word, or just another sniveling little NSA asshole who wants to give me excuses about needing more time. You don't need more time, you just need to grow a pair and give me what I'm asking for, and you're going to do it today."

Riker let out a long, low sigh as his head fell back against the limo's rear seat headrest.

"Why are you so invested in finding out what may or may not be happening with that plane, Ray? Do you have an operative on there? Is all of this about trying to protect your team? Whatever it is that you're involved in?"

Tilley again considered a response, and again decided to simply tell Riker the truth.

"Yeah, I do have one of mine on that plane. Actually, he's being considered for the program. It was my idea that he take some time off while I try to get him approved."

Bradley Riker's eyes indicated his increasing understanding of why Tilley was so willing to try and save a man who was not yet even part of his team.

"So you were the one who unwittingly put him on the missing plane."

Tilley nodded once as he looked to his right and saw a large, black SUV pull up in the other lane next to the limo.

"Yeah, I am."

"I assume you've had a few others die on your watch, Ray. What makes this guy so special?"

This was something Ray Tilley wasn't ready to share with Riker, or anyone else for that matter. His interest in Mac Walker went beyond thinking him as merely another valuable asset to the program. There was something about Walker that led Tilley to believe the former Navy SEAL had a destiny far beyond, and far greater, than Project Icon. Call it a hunch, intuition, or even a whispered suggestion from the Almighty, Ray Tilley believed Mac Walker would one day somehow play a pivotal role in helping to save them all.

"Just get me the information I've asked for, Bradley. I'm dropping you off at your home. Go inside and do what you got to do to bring me that information later today. I'll contact you again in three hours."

While Riker exited the limo on his way back to his apartment, Ray Tilley looked down at his watch. In three hours it would be almost four o'clock. Hopefully, that would leave him enough time to figure out what the hell was going on with Mac Walker and that missing plane.

Until then, he had no choice but to simply wait.

17.

The priest hated these meetings. The Vatican was one long, unending meeting. Robed men scurrying about, nodding, sly smiles, knowing eyes…and the damned meetings.

Father Barnes wanted to get as far away from Rome as he possibly could, back to his medical studies, his cancer research. The Jesuit Order he had devoted his life to, demanded he now remain here though until this mess with the missing plane be resolved. There were whispers of a plot against the church, perhaps even an imminent assassination attempt. And so, the Vatican sent for Father Barnes and his somewhat unique skill set. That, and the fact Victor Barnes knew Stasia Wellington, and the church feared Stasia had gone rogue. She had been out of communication for over a week with no indications of whether she remained dead, or alive.

Father Barnes knew an operative like Stasia would prove exceedingly difficult to kill, so he remained convinced she was out there, up to *something*. What that something was, he didn't yet know.

"Victor, you do not appear pleased to be here today. Is there anything I can do to make you more comfortable?"

Cardinal Copilli's heavily lidded eyes reminded Father Barnes of how a snake might gaze at the rat just before clamping its mouth around the wretched creature and swallowing it whole. The cardinal was among the most powerful figures within the church hierarchy, a man whose counsel went directly to the pope himself. Some even believed the pope feared Cardinal Copilli more than he feared God. Such was the scope of the cardinal's position as head of Vatican Intelligence.

"You can make me more comfortable by allowing me to go back home to Maryland. My research is my primary interest these days Cardinal. Of course, you already know that."

The fifty-seven year old Cardinal Copilli smiled back at Father Barnes, his thin lipped mouth slashing across the lean, almost gaunt face while the reptilian eyes remained absent any warmth.

"Need I remind you that your position at the hospital, and your subsequent research there, is due in great part to the support and approval of the church, Father Barnes?"

I could jump across this table and snap the man's neck like a dried out chicken bone.

"I always figured it was my family's money that was primarily responsible for that Cardinal Copilli – no offense to the church of course."

Father Barnes watched with well hidden satisfaction as he saw the cardinal's eyes flash with indignation at having someone of such low ranking as Victor Barnes speak to him with such seeming indifference.

"Be that as it may Father, I would remind you that the hospital you spend so much time at, is a *Catholic* hospital. I would also point out that the time this church has invested in your development, requires that you honor that investment by doing what is asked of you, when it is asked of you. Now is such a time. There are those here who fear for the safety of the Vatican itself, and I am personally convinced your former student, Stasia Wellington, is a central figure in whatever threat is being perpetrated against us."

"Stasia wouldn't harm the church. She wouldn't harm innocents."

Cardinal Copilli shifted himself in the large, leather bound chair that sat behind the massive and ornate oak desk that likely dated back at least three centuries. The cardinal's office was said to have once been the private library of Pope Pius II, who had led the church in the mid-1400's. It wasn't necessarily a large space, but every inch of it was ornately carved, crafted, and constructed from an era dating back nearly a thousand years ago. Rich, deep purple tapestries hung from dark wooded walls that met a gold flecked ceiling. The artwork alone positioned throughout the office was invaluable, including a genuine Botticelli sketch the predated that author's famous *Map of Hell* painting used for Dante's *Divine Comedy*.

The faint, sickly-sweet smell of burning incense permeated the office, a scent that always made Father Barnes feel slightly nauseous.

"How do you know that, Father Barnes? Why are you so certain of Stasia's devotion to the church?"

He's trying to determine if I'm helping her – if I'm part of the plot.

"So you want to question my loyalties too Cardinal, is that it? I already told you everything I know about Stasia Wellington. She is a highly intelligent, very capable operative, and someone I wouldn't care to insult."

Cardinal Copilli pursed his lips while folding his thin fingered hands under his chin.

"Then what was she doing on that plane, Father Barnes? She was not authorized by this church to do so. And now that plane has gone missing."

Victor Barnes held up his hands and shrugged. It had been nearly a decade since he had trained Stasia, and that was shortly before he left Vatican Intelligence to devote himself entirely to his medical research.

"I don't know, Cardinal, I haven't been involved in this shit for a long time now. This is your world, not mine. You want to know what Stasia Wellington was doing on that plane, I suggest you get off your ass and try to find out yourself."

Cardinal Copilli's cheeks flushed an angry red, matching the color of the worn vestment favored by the highest ranking church officials.

"I don't approve of your insolence, Father Barnes. Profanity is a sign of a weak and ignorant mind, to say nothing about your unkempt appearance. When is the last time you had a shave?"

Father Barnes chuckled.

"You really think God gives two shits about a potty mouth or some facial growth?"

The cardinal's right hand slammed down onto his desk.

"Enough! You will not speak that way inside of this office! I am your superior, Father Barnes! You answer to *me*, and I answer to God!"

Father Barnes leaned back in his chair opposite the cardinal and folded his heavily muscled forearms across his chest.

"Now hold on, Cardinal, I get that I have to answer to you, but I thought that you answered to the Sancta Sedes - the Holy Father our pope, and *he* answers to God. Or do I have that wrong somehow?"

The former crimson red of the cardinal's cheeks burned a darker hue as outright rage filled his eyes. His words hissed across the desk toward Father Barnes, who sat unimpressed.

"I am scheduling a full inquiry into your involvement in this matter, Father Barnes. You have an hour to prepare for questioning. I suggest you take a moment to pray for forgiveness, as clearly, you are a lamb gone far astray from the flock."

The priest's deep, rough voice issued forth in an ominous, low growl.

"I eat lamb, Cardinal, and I've never been one for following the flock. Instead of wasting time trying to intimidate me, questioning me, or whatever else you have in mind, how about you just get me all the information you already have on that missing plane, and let me see if I can put together a more legitimate idea of what might be happening, because it's become all too clear during what little time we've spent talking here, that you couldn't find your own ass from a hole in the dirt."

Cardinal Copilli sat unmoving in his chair. Even his eyes refused to blink as he watched in silence as Father Victor Barnes stood up and made his way toward the door of the study. Finally, just as Father Barnes extended a hand to pull the door open, the cardinal's voice spoke just loud enough to be heard across the room.

"I've been told the American FDA has concerns over your research, Father, though they have hesitated from acting on that concern out of respect for the church. It would be a shame to see that hesitation dissipate, and your life's work effectively shut down. Your full and respectful cooperation in the matter of the missing plane might lessen that unfortunate possibility from happening."

Father Barnes was not one to accept threats with indifference, but he also knew his medical work did enjoy a certain degree of protection through his affiliation with the Catholic Church, protection that he very much wanted to continue to be the recipient of to ensure his research would continue – research he believed would save lives otherwise lost to the disease of cancer. He knew that he must, in essence, suffer the figurative cancer that infected the bureaucracy of the church, in order to protect himself from the potentially more aggressive, bureaucratic cancer of the American government.

Without looking back, he let the cardinal know the less than subtle threat was both received, and fully understood.

"Get me the information you have on the missing plane Cardinal, and I give you my word to do my best to find out what's going on."

18.

Bradley Riker appeared literally ready to jump out of his skin. Ray Tilley had assumed the time constraints he placed on his longtime NSA informant would prove difficult, but apparently, it was just about breaking the poor bastard.

It was just over three hours since last they spoke in the back of the limo. Now they sat across from one another at a roadside diner some twenty miles north of Washington D.C. on Route 108. Tilley knew D.C. politicos didn't do roadside diners, so the chance of being seen by anyone from that world was all but nil.

"You don't know what this cost me Tilley. I have my entire ass hanging out on this one."

Riker's voice was a seething whisper, his eyes looking toward the diner door and then back to Tilley, a layer of sweat covering the entirety of his forehead as his lightly folded hands trembled in front of him where they sat atop an unmarked manila folder.

"This thing has people way up in the food chain asking questions. I'm talking Defense, NSA, Interpol, the French government, the Italians, I was told there are lobbyists from Atlantis Airlines meeting at the White House this afternoon. What have you gotten yourself into Ray? What the hell have you gotten *me* into?"

Ray Tilley had never seen Riker so agitated over intelligence data, confirming his earlier feeling that both General Tinney and Mardian had been less than forthcoming on what was really involved with Flight 444's disappearance.

Tilley sat silently, waiting patiently for Riker to hand over the just compiled intelligence file. Bradley Riker, knowing there would be no more information forthcoming from his former college roommate, slid the file across the table and then glanced once again toward the door.

"That's it, I'm done, Tilley. No more calls, no more meetings, you are on your own. We're square now, right? Even if I somehow manage to get out of this with my career intact, if you want information, you need to find someone else to get it for you."

Ray Tilley gave a short nod but said nothing, his attention already focused on the contents of the file. He barely noted Riker's departure from the diner, as his eyes came first to the section detailing the woman known as Stasia Wellington.

Bosnian born, her original surname had been Kavik, but the family changed their name to Wellington shortly after arriving in London in the late 1980's when Stasia was still a teenager. The Kaviks were Catholic, meaning that during their time in Bosnia, were among a distinct minority and likely often persecuted by the Muslim majority of that small nation who outnumbered Catholics by ten to one.

Soon after her nineteenth birthday, Stasia Wellington entered the Holy Trinity Monastery to begin her formation process to becoming a nun. It was at that point her file indicated an absence of information for nearly three years, until she again appeared as an operations manager for a Catholic monastery in Washington D.C. where she remained for just over a year. Then her timeline went blank once again until she reappeared two years later as a consultant for the Vatican Public Relations Office, where, if Riker's information was correct, she remained to present day.

This information mirrored that of the file General Tinny had shared with Tilley during their meeting earlier that day. Stasia Wellington was an active operative within the Vatican Intelligence Service, her position as a "consultant" simply a title to afford her anonymity within the vast, multi-layered tiers of Vatican government.

Directly below the section devoted to Stasia was a black and white photograph of a broad shouldered man in his early 40's named Victor Barnes, a medical doctor and Jesuit priest who was listed as an instructor to Stasia during her time in Washington D.C.

Following the pages devoted to Stasia Wellington were several more outlining the missing plane's flight crew. First was Captain David Rogers, formerly David Kurjak. Like Stasia, his family originated from Bosnia, and like Stasia, he too had been London educated before moving full time to the United States. He had been a pilot for two decades, and worked for Atlantis Airlines since 1996, shortly after changing his last name from Kurjak to Rogers.

It was also in 1996 that Rogers had taken a three week vacation to travel to Switzerland where he attended a conference by a controversial Muslim cleric named Torgal Al-Muhamed. Tilley knew the name well. The seventy three year old Torgal Al-Muhamed had publicly declared his approval of the 9-11 bombings from his mosque in Baden, Switzerland just hours after the tragedy took place.

The fact both the U.S. government and Atlantis Airlines were allowing Rogers to continue flying planes even after his relatively recent interest in the works of a clearly radical, terrorist supporting Muslim cleric, made Ray Tilley clench his jaw in frustration.

Political correctness will be the death of us all.

The co-pilot's name was Frederick Anderson, a thirty nine year old former Air Force fighter pilot who had joined Atlantis Airlines two years earlier after retiring from the Air Force. Born in Atlanta, Georgia, he had enlisted just two months out of high school. Anderson was married with three kids. Nothing in the report suggested any connection to terrorist groups, or a previous relationship to either Captain Rogers or Stasia Wellington.

The two female flight attendants were another matter. Each one, like the pilot and Stasia Wellington, were Bosnian. Tilley scanned over the picture of an attractive blonde named Danika, who had been working for Atlantis since 1999, and a somewhat older, brown haired woman named Milla, who had been with the airline for almost seven years. In the right margin next to each of the women's photo was a handwritten note from Riker:

Both women's families originate from same Bosnian village as pilot.

Other than the link to the same village as Captain Rogers, there was no evidence in the report to suggest either woman had any affiliations to terrorist groups.

The other flight attendant was male, and had no connection to Bosnia. His name was Walter Hill, a white male in his early 30's, born in Boston, who attended a year of junior college in upstate New York. Hill then worked several odd jobs for a number of years before being hired by Atlantis Airlines just four months ago.

The next page in Riker's report was devoted entirely to the air marshal assigned to Atlantis Flight 444 - Reyos Huskich. Huskich maintained the Bosnian link, though unlike the others, he had direct experience as a member of the U.N. peace keeping mission during the Bosnian Conflict, likely exposing him to some of the most brutal atrocities committed during that brief, but very intense war between various ethnic groups. Reyos was born an American citizen, was a veteran of the U.S. military, and had been accepted into the air marshal program three years earlier.

Another hand written note was left by Riker:

Live in same Huntington Beach neighborhood - predominantly Bosniak-Muslim street. Attend same mosque. Attended same Torgal Al-Muhamed conference in '96 as did Capt. Rogers.

Next to the handwritten note was a photograph of Torgal Al-Muhamed attending a June, 2001 fundraising event with the head of the New York based Allah's Children Group, a highly influential political action committee that generated millions of dollars in donations to numerous political campaigns across the country during each election cycle, dating back to the 1970's. Tilley had researched the organization shortly after the September 11th attacks, and found nearly half of their fundraising dollars originated from Saudi donors.

Those dollars then found their way into the campaign coffers of the current Senate Majority Leader, House Speaker, and the President of the United States.

So this is what got Riker so spooked. Can't say I blame him. These are some mighty powerful sacred cows who sure as hell don't want to look as if they have anything to do with the people who might have hijacked that missing plane.

As good as this information from Riker was, it still left Tilley without any idea as to what Atlantis Flight 444's flight crew intended to do with the plane, if in fact they did take it over. Where would they go? And more importantly, why?

Ray Tilley heard his phone vibrating on the diner table, its screen indicating a number he had never seen before. It was his Project Icon phone, and normally the only call that ever came in on it was from Stephen Mardian.

"This is Tilley – who is this?"

There was a slight pause before a deep, roughened voice answered.

"Mr. Tilley, my name is Father Victor Barnes. I believe it might do us both some good if you and I had ourselves a little talk."

19.

Captain Rogers and Air Marshal Huskich walked confidently down the just delivered boarding steps, each man looking at the tallest of the four men who stood waiting for them on the ground.

Colonel Imed Mabazza was a serious man undertaking serious business, considered by many in his country of Tunisia to be that nation's true kingmaker. Colonel Mabazza had, over the last ten years, consolidated his authority over much of the Tunisian military, and provided protection to various international corporations who utilized the nation as an essential money laundering facility. This was done for a price of course, a price that had made the colonel a very wealthy man.

Now nearing his sixtieth year, Colonel Mabazza grew impatient. Beyond the duties of business, were the increasingly urgent spiritual demands that he knew must be promoted. Following the glorious attacks upon the American Satan on 9-11, Allah would be glorified even further by an attack on perhaps humankind's greatest devil, the Catholic beast whose shadow originated from the cesspool that was the Vatican. It had been nearly twenty years when Mabazza, then a lowly private, had initiated the first of what would be a great many executions of non-Muslims throughout his nation. Since that time, no fewer than eighty such executions had taken place, some of them under his own knife.

Today though, was to be no simple knife across the throat of an infidel, but rather a thunderous retribution long overdue against the Catholic horde. One that would initiate an all too predictable reaction – the panicked need for more weaponry as Muslims killed Christians, and nations then prepared for war. Colonel Mabazza and his Saudi connections would then sell to all sides, as their influence expanded as quickly and greatly as their wealth.

The "peace keepers" would be their most profitable clients of course, that gaping hole that was the United Nations into which the foolish behemoths like the United States poured billions of dollars into. Dollars that would then be used to destroy the behemoth through ever increasing global regulations, trading inequalities, and of course, more wars. It was, at long last, the beginnings of a New United Nations, upon which a conclusion would resolve itself to banish, once and for all, the American experiment that had always been doomed for failure.

"Colonel Mabazza, you honor us with your presence, sir. As you can see, we have delivered the plane, and are ready to deliver the weapon you promised us."

The colonel dipped his head slightly toward Captain Rogers, and then extended his right hand toward a simple, small wooden structure outside of which two armed Tunisian soldiers stood.

"Right this way, gentlemen. Let us get out of this hot sun and discuss what happens next."

Reyos Huskich walked behind both the captain and the colonel, noting the colonel's immaculate, light green military suit and shoes that were polished to a brilliant sheen. Colonel Mabazza appeared to be at least a couple inches over six feet, his lean frame and posture perfectly straight, his walk the movements of a man supremely confident in his control over the world around him. And despite approaching sixty, the colonel's dark skin was almost completely devoid of lines. He appeared quite capable of living another two decades or more.

Once inside the structure, the colonel sat down at a small metallic desk and instructed the other two men to take make use of the chairs opposite him.

"Welcome to my office abroad. It is here I have conducted some of the most important transactions of my career. Today is perhaps *the* most important of all of them. What we intend to do with that plane will be spoken of through the ages, long after all of us are gone."

At that moment the air marshal concluded he had no patience for the preening Tunisian colonel. The man's self importance annoyed Reyos Huskich, who simply wanted their business concluded so the plane could once again be on its way to the Vatican.
"Where is the weapon and the fuel?"

Captain Roger's glared at the Huskich, worried the man had offended the colonel. Colonel Mabazza merely smiled, and tilted his head toward the open door of the hut.

"Both are being delivered to the island as we speak. I have a ship 500 yards from this location. You did not expect me to take the risk of moving such a unique weapon until I knew you would be here, did you? And the plane will be refueled, yes, that is being delivered as well, more than enough to complete your journey."

"There is no rescue operation in the area, correct?"

The colonel nodded, the thin smile remaining on his smooth skinned face.

"All attention has been diverted to the debris field you left a thousand miles from here. The media are making much of the fact the plane's automated communications system was shut off, but speculation is that the impact of the crash may have caused that, or a significant malfunction. We are, for now, completely hidden from their rescue operation. Plus, should their attention turn to this area, the Tunisian government would of course provide assistance in the search, and since I am much of what constitutes the Tunisian government…"

Colonel Mabazza's voice trailed off, the man's overwhelming confidence in himself once again annoying Huskich.

"Oh, and what of the passengers, gentlemen? I want no bloodshed on my island, so if you intend to kill them, please do so on the plane. I am happy to provide you weapons, as I assume the only armed member of your crew is the air marshal here, and he could not have afforded to waste ammunition so soon in the mission, correct?"

Captain Rogers nodded his head in gratitude.

"Yes, we'd be grateful for more weapons Colonel, though I intend to keep the passengers alive to the very end of our journey. I want the infidels' fears to be another gift to Allah, as they realize where we are going, and what we intend to do."

Colonel Mabazza stared intently at the captain for a moment before rising from behind the desk.

"Very well then, I believe I hear the arrival of the weapon and your fuel."

Once again the captain and air marshal followed behind the colonel as he strode toward the surrounding beach in the direction of a single, steel hulled military transport boat that had beached itself. Despite his annoyance with the Tunisian military peacock named Mabazza, Reyos Huskich could barely contain his anticipation over the completion of the mission. Soon, the world would know his name. Soon, the world would be forever changed.

The air marshal looked over to the hangar structure, confident the gun he had left with Milla would be enough to keep the cowardly passengers in line until he returned to the plane. Just before departing with the captain, Danika had informed him the American army boy remained bound in one of the bathrooms to the homosexual, both men still unconscious.

All was going according to Allah's divine plan.

20.

"Go ahead, Father Barnes, you have my full attention."

Ray Tilley kept his voice low, not wanting anyone else in the nearly empty diner to overhear the phone conversation.

"Mackenzie Walker, Mr. Tilley – why was he on Atlantis Flight 444?"

Tilley glanced over at the diner entrance and then leaned down toward the table, his voice lowering even further.

"How about you start by telling me why Stasia Wellington was on that same flight?"

Tilley was surprised at the absence of hesitation from Father Barnes, thinking his mentioning of Wellington would catch the priest by surprise.

"I don't know Mr. Tilley, I haven't had a say in Stasia's whereabouts for a very long time. I don't believe that same fact applies regarding you and Mr. Walker though."

Ray Tilley stood up and made his way quickly toward the exit, wanting to continue the conversation outside.

"He's not one of ours, if that's what you're thinking Father Barnes, at least, not yet. So tell me, are you calling on behalf of Vatican Intelligence, because I was told they'd already struck a deal with the American government, and representatives for the airline – that officially, Mac Walker and Stasia Wellington were never on that plane."

Tilley grinned as he realized this time he did catch the priest off guard.

"Is that right? And who told you that?"

"Probably the same people who allowed you to get this number Father Barnes. How about we cut to the chase here – what do you want?"

"I want some goddamn answers, Mr. Tilley. Whatever happened to that missing plane has some very important people around here worried, and they're chewing on my ass to find out what your man was doing on that flight. Now the way I figure it, you have the same kind of self important assholes on your end of things, pushing you to give them answers too, am I right?"

This is one angrily aggressive, foul mouthed priest.

"Yeah, Father that sounds about right."

During the next ten minutes, each man shared the information the other had regarding the missing plane, the connections among the flight crew, the links to and the possibility the plane had been hijacked and was being hidden at an unknown location somewhere. There was little that one man knew that wasn't already known by the other, with the sole exception of the priest indicating high ranking officials in Rome believed an attack might be imminent on the Vatican itself.

Tilley assumed then those same officials believed the missing 767 was to be used as some kind of delivery device, similar to what took place so recently in New York on September 11th, 2001.

The debris pile off the coast of France could be an intentional distraction.

"Father Barnes, if a plane were hijacked from France, to later be used as a weapon against the Vatican, what area would provide the hijackers the greatest opportunity for success?"

Tilley could hear the priest clearing his throat before responding.

"They wouldn't fly over the European continent, far too many surveillance systems in place to go undetected, anti missile defense systems, etc."

Tilley nodded his head.

"That's right – they'd be coming from across the Mediterranean. Now with that in mind, are there any other governments in the area that come to mind who would want to initiate such an aggressive attack on the Vatican?"

The priest grunted on the other end.

"Take your pick, Mr. Tilley, as you well know, it's a dangerous world. There are factions within Morocco, Algeria, Tunisia, Libya, Egypt…"

"I'm not asking you about groups of militants or dissidents who dislike Rome, Father. I'm asking what governments in the area could, and would, be willing to pull something like this off? Eliminate both Morocco and Egypt. Both are too far from a direct flight line into Rome. That leaves Algeria, Tunisia, and Libya. Libya is too obvious, and for as unbalanced as he appears, Gaddafi knows that. He wouldn't involve himself in this, at least not directly.

"So that leaves us with Algeria and Tunisia. Both offer the possibility of a direct flight path into Rome without having to cross land to get there, with Tunisia being both the shortest, and most direct. Both nations suffer from radical Islamic elements that are rampant throughout all levels of their government. I suggest we focus on those two countries to see if we can uncover anything that might indicate where the plane could have been taken, if it was in fact taken. I also suggest we be very quick about it Father Barnes, because if Atlantis Flight 444 is being used as a weapon, it would take that craft no more than an hour to fly from North Africa to Rome, and I have a distinct feeling we are running out of time."

The priest went silent for several seconds before his baritone growl resumed the conversation.

"Perhaps we need to see if there are any links between the cleric Torgal Al-Muhamed and anyone within the Algerian or Tunisian governments? That could be the thread that ties all of this together."

Ray Tilley's eyes widened as he stood outside the diner with the Project Icon phone to his ear, sensing the priest's suggestion held merit, while also disappointed he had not come more quickly to that same conclusion himself.

"I'm on it, Father Barnes. Check in again within the hour. Oh, and one more thing. You mind telling me how you came to have this number?"

The priest ended the call without an answer.

It took both men no more than forty minutes to locate the link between the radical Muslim cleric Torgal Al-Muhamed and the Tunisian government, though in Tilley's defense, half that time was devoted to his returning back from the roadside diner to his home office in the D.C. suburbs. This link centered on the same June 2001 Allah's Children Group fundraiser that Bradley Riker had included in his intelligence report to Ray Tilley earlier that day, based off of a New York Times article of the event, an article Tilley was now looking at on his computer. Among the dignitaries at that event was one Colonel Imed Mabazza, a military strongman who had long been a fixture in the upper echelons of Tunisian government.

Tilley's phone rang. Before he had a chance to speak, the priest's voice cut across the thousands of miles that separated them.

"Tunisia. If that plane was taken, it's in Tunisia. You see the New York Times story on the fundraiser from last year, the picture of the cleric and Colonel Mabazza standing together?"

Ray Tilley clicked on the image so that it covered his entire screen.

"Yeah, looking at it right now."

Tilley looked down at the photograph and found himself staring into the eyes of the colonel, noting how dark and devoid of emotion they were. They were certainly the eyes of a man capable of inflicting great pain onto others.

"So what now, Mr. Tilley?"

Ray Tilley clicked off the New York Times link.

"I'm gonna see if I can get some one of our ships located in the Mediterranean to scramble a couple fighter jets along the Tunisian coast, try and locate the plane. We'll pull up satellite data, make unofficial inquiries into the Tunisian government, and hope to god our hunch is wrong. What about you, Father? Can the Vatican get the Italian military to be put on alert status?"

"Probably, but they still want to believe the plane is most likely under a thousand feet of water off the French coast. And…there's something else to consider too."

Tilley already knew what the priest was referring to.

"There's the matter of Stasia and your Mr. Walker. If that plane was hijacked, and they've managed to stay alive, they're gonna fight back. At least, I know Stasia will. If there's any way possible to keep that plane from being used as a weapon, she'll make it happen."

Ray Tilley was nodding to himself. He had already thought that very thing regarding Mac Walker's own seemingly limitless determination to never give up, and never give in.

21.

"So that's it? I expected something more…imposing."

Colonel Imed Mabazza lifted the small metallic tube from the transport box and held it up in his hands.

"I assure you captain, just this one canister is enough to wipe out every living thing within a half mile of the detonation point. We are delivering twenty-two such canisters for your flight to Rome. No-one within the Vatican will survive this attack, and their suffering will be excruciating."

"What is it?"

The air marshal was even more dubious of the colonel's claim than was the captain, his eyes looking over the rows of identical canisters lined up inside of the transport bin.

Colonel Mabazza returned the canister with the others and then smiled down at Reyos Huskich.

"It is a v-series nerve agent more commonly called Purple Possum, Mr. Huskich. Developed by the British in the 1950's, and quickly banned by international authorities shortly thereafter. I have a scientist who has been modifying it, enhancing its properties to allow it to be more easily spread, and thus, giving it an even greater dispersion. It kills both by skin contact, and even more quickly, via intrusion into the lungs. The victim effectively drowns in their own fluids. Normally it would take nearly ten milligrams to kill a human being. We have lowered that amount to just five. All of these canisters combined will deliver over ten thousand milligrams. Your plane is being refueled, and with Rome being just an hour's flight away, will remain nearly full of fuel upon its arrival, thus ensuring a rather significant detonation, which in turn will allow the nerve agent to be spread several miles around that detonation point. All you need do is place this box as close to the fuselage as possible. It will make the Twin Towers attack in America look like child's play compared to the tens of thousands who will die at your hand, and those thousands will of course be inhabitants of that den of sin – the Vatican itself. We shall remove the head from the Christian blight that darkens this world."

Huskich was now smiling as his eyes looked over the canisters with near manic hunger, his initial annoyance toward the colonel now forgotten as his mind filled itself with the imagined images of the death and destruction he would deliver to Rome. Allah would most certainly reward him well in the afterlife for such a deed.

Captain Rogers looked toward the hanger as a pressurized portable fuel container was being put in place just under the 767.

"How long before we are ready for departure colonel?"

Colonel Mabazza followed the captain's gaze to the hanger.

"Very soon now, Captain Rogers. Twenty minutes to refuel, and then I will have the canisters placed inside of your cargo hold. From there, you are free to go, and may Allah's vengeance be with you."

At the very moment Colonel Mabazza was blessing Captain Rogers with Allah's vengeance, Mac Walker was peering out a window at the very back of the 767 as the fuel container was moved under the plane.

"They're refueling the plane - two armed men below us."

Mac looked back at Walter, who in turn was keeping watch for any sign of Milla, who they suspected had been left with the air marshal's weapon.

"Walter, how long does a typical refueling take given the estimated fuel burn that's already happened based on a flight from Paris to somewhere off the coast of Northern Africa?"

"We should still have half our fuel capacity left Mac, so no more than twenty, maybe thirty minutes."

Mac considered the implications of the refuel. The plane could have made the relatively short crossing to Rome with the fuel it already had. Topping off the tanks confirmed for the former Navy SEAL that the 767 was in fact being used as a weapon – the more fuel, the bigger the explosion and resulting carnage.

Mac looked out the small window once again, catching a glimpse of blue waters in the distance.

Let them refuel the plane, we might need it once we fly out of here.

Mac had decided to take back the 767. He wasn't sure how just yet, given he and the others were without weapons, and now appeared to be surrounded by armed soldiers. Just how many armed soldiers was another question that remained unanswered.

Those uniforms – I recognize them!

"We're in Tunisia. That's Tunisian military out there."

Mac had spent nine days in 1998 with a contingent of other navy SEALS and NATO officials monitoring a suspected arms dealer who worked the border between Tunisia and Libya. That arms dealer also happened to be Tunisian military – a colonel by the name of Mabazza. After those nine days, Mac's team was ordered to pull out of the area. No reason was given, and the operation was never mentioned to him again.

Stasia leaned her head into Mac's to allow her to look outside the plane as well. She then nodded her head.

"You're right, definitely Tunisian military, just as I suspected."

Mac stood up and stared down at the Vatican Intelligence agent.

"Suspected? So your being on this plane *is* part of a mission?"

Stasia moved past Mac and into the food prep room where he followed closely behind her.

"No, Mr. Walker I'm not on a mission, I'm on a hunch. My being here isn't official Vatican business. I have been monitoring airline activity even before September 11th, reviewing airline personnel files, travel records, affiliations, and over time, my instincts pointed me to Captain David Rogers, formerly, David Kurjak. Bosnian-American, with family who had been slaughtered during the Bosnian war ten years ago. I took my suspicions to my superiors, and was shut down. In fact, they said I was overworked, overly paranoid, and needed to take some time off.

"So, I took their advice and left the Vatican, instead tracking Captain Rogers' flights personally. This is the third time in the last month I've been on a plane he is piloting. Guess the third time really is the charm, huh? Now knowing how the Vatican works, my guess is they are now panicking after this plane went missing, and they learned Rogers was the pilot, realizing I might have been right after all. Or, maybe they think I'm actually in on it. They're more than stupid enough to go that route too."

Mac knew the feeling well. His own attitude regarding Washington D.C.'s bureaucracy was much the same as Stasia's toward the Vatican's.

"Milla is coming! She has the gun!"

Walter's whispered warning averted Mac's attention away from Stasia and toward the front of the plane. A few paces behind Milla was Danika, whose eyes were straining to catch a glimpse of Mac or the others at the back of the plane.

"You! You there! Are you trying to use your phone? Idiot! You think I'm that stupid! Damn Americans with your phones and your arrogance! You won't get a signal, we're blocking it. All of your phones are useless inside this plane."

Milla loomed over the young black man who earlier sat across from Mac, the man's cell phone held between his bound hands. The flight attendant's face was contorted into a grotesque image of mocking confidence, her eyes gleaming with excitement as she held the tip of the air marshal's gun against the passenger's left temple.

"Disgusting little ape, aren't you?"

Mac knew the flight attendant's tone all too well – she was preparing to kill the passenger. Something in her wanted badly to take a life, wanted to experience the power of doing so.

He stood nearly twenty feet from Milla, the food prep area's thin blue curtain the only thing separating him from the main cabin and the business end of the handgun the deranged flight attendant held in her hand.

Even for a man capable of considerable speed and power, as Mac was, twenty feet was quite a distance when one's opponent was armed and ready to shoot – perhaps too much distance. That left the former Navy SEAL with but one option to increase his chances for success.

Mac Walker reached for a bag of peanuts.

22.

"Father Barnes, what you are implying is outrageous, and frankly, I fear it's an attempt to divert attention, and blame, away from Stasia Wellington. While I admire your loyalty to her, I suggest you reacquaint yourself to the loyalty you owe the church. You cannot expect me to call up the Italian president with this nonsense. What you have described is a plot in some spy thriller movie, not real life! I'll be laughed out of Rome!"

Victor Barnes took a deliberately slow, measured breath as he found himself back in the cardinal's Vatican office. The priest had expected the cardinal to react to the possibility of the Tunisian plot this way. The man was a politician, always looking to protect and better his position within the church power structure.

"You asked me to find out what was going on with that missing plane Cardinal Copilli. I believe I've done that. You worry about being laughed out of Rome? What if I'm right, and thousands are killed because of your failure to act accordingly? I've shown you the links between the cleric, the flight crew, and a high ranking member of the Tunisian government. Yes, there's still some space between one leading to the other, but given we may very well be running out of time, don't you think it prudent to at least prepare? Call up the president, inform him of the possible plot, and let the government do what a government is supposed to do – protect its people."

The cardinal's eyes looked downward toward the top of his desk, where they remained for some time. When those eyes lifted to once again stare back at the priest, Father Barnes knew the cardinal would make the call, though his motivation was far more likely to be a case of self preservation than it was an opportunity to do the right thing.

"Very well Victor, I will contact the defense liaison to the president, and inform him of your theory, but know this – it will be *your* name attached to this, not mine. I am acting merely as a messenger."

Father Barnes stood up while nodding down at the cardinal.

"I don't give a shit about whose name is attached to what Cardinal, I just want to do everything I can to make sure innocent lives are saved. Give me the blame, or you take the credit, whatever gets you off, man. Just make that call, and make it quick."

At the very moment Father Barnes walked out of Cardinal Copilli's office, Ray Tilley found himself seated across from both General Tinny and Stephen Mardian in the same Pentagon conference room he had met with them earlier.

"Tunisia? That's what you've come up with? The plane was taken to Tunisia? And you came up with this shit working with some priest in the Vatican? Are you aware of the most recent flight details Mr. Tilley? That 767 was flying erratically before it disappeared. It ascended, then descended, and most likely smashed itself to bits in the Atlantic Ocean. Everything points to some kind of catastrophic failure. It's a tragedy, but not a conspiracy. 217 lives have been lost, including your Mr. Walker. Maybe you don't want to accept that, you've come up with this outlandish bullshit, but there is no way I take this to anyone else outside this conference room. I already told you, we've initiated some clean up regarding Walker and Wellington's presence on the plane. Other than that, I consider this event a tragedy, nothing more, and certainly not something we need to waste any more of our time on."

General Tinny rose from his chair and then paused as Stephen Mardian looked up at the Pentagon veteran.

"Sit down, General."

The general's eyes widened as he stood over Mardian, who in turn was calmly looking over at Tilley.

"You don't order *me*, Mardian."

Stephen Mardian lightly brushed something from the left sleeve of his suit jacket and smiled.

"Let's not pretend right now, General. I think Mr. Tilley's concerns may hold merit. I think it would be prudent, at the very least, for you to give a heads up to our military presence throughout the Mediterranean. Perhaps a quick call to the State Department, see if they have anything that might clarify a possible Tunisian connection."

The skin around General Tinny's fleshy face transformed into a collection of mottled reds and purples, as he jabbed a stubby finger toward Mardian's chest.

"I will do no such thing! Christ, Mardian, do you know the questions that will be raised if I march out of here and start crying wolf based on this asshole's weightless premise of some Tunisian conspiracy! Project Icon is not your toy. That plane is gone, understand? We have a debris field, lost communication, erratic flight pattern moments before it disappeared – Atlantis Flight 444 is not sitting somewhere in Tunisia for god's sake! It's at the bottom of the goddamn ocean!"

Stephen Mardian leaned back in his chair and stared up at the still standing General Tinny.

"But what if he's right, General? You'll likely be brought up on charges for failing to notify. Call it chatter, a hunch, whatever you need to do to keep your own hands clean, but Mr. Tilley has shown us enough that we must, at the very least, forward the possibility to those who might be in a position to act. I'm giving you an opportunity right now to do it your way. If you refuse, that leaves me no choice but to do it my way, and that will leave you looking like you're participation in Project Icon is of negligible importance, General Tinny. Is that the perception you wish to have known by others?"

The general's mouth slashed downward as his nostrils flared open, his eyes glowering down at the lobbyist, knowing Mardian's power and influence within Washington D.C. was likely far greater than his own.

"Sit down."

This time Tinny did as Mardian asked, lowering himself back into his chair where he remained silently awaiting Mardian's instructions.

"Thank you, General. Now, as I said, I think it wise for you to use whatever channels you deem appropriate to let U.S. military interests closest to North Africa know that there may be a quickly developing threat coming from that region. No need to get too specific if that concerns you, just a basic heads up. No harm in that, right?"

The general said nothing, his eyes staring back at Stephen Mardian who appeared even more at ease than he had been earlier.

"As for you, Mr. Tilley, there is to be no further communication with your Vatican source. Let them handle things on their end as they choose, just as we will do on ours, do you understand?"

Ray Tilley gave a brief nod, though privately, he had no intention of allowing Mardian to dictate to him who he could speak to.

"Very well then, gentlemen it seems we've come to something of a conclusion, for now. General, I look forward to a full report first thing tomorrow morning. Mr. Tilley, you can go. Please give me and the general a moment alone. Thank you."

Tilley walked to the conference room door and began closing it behind him, then paused to look up at Stephen Mardian, who in turn sat staring back at Tilley, his eyes unblinking, the hint of a smile marking his face.

It was the smile of a man Ray Tilley knew could never fully be trusted.

23.

Mac Walker held the pack of peanuts in his right hand, preparing to throw them at Milla's head before she fired the gun, and hoping it would startle the flight attendant enough to allow him time to disarm her. Then again, he also knew her trigger finger might instead instinctively squeeze off a round into the young man's head.

She's gonna kill him either way, so this is the only chance he's got.

Mac's hand propelled the peanuts toward Milla, the packet colliding with the right side of her forehead. The flight attendant's head snapped to the left a few inches while at the same time, Mac sprang from behind the curtain like a tiger pouncing onto its prey.

Milla recovered quickly, but not quite quickly enough.

Mac Walker's left shoulder slammed into her side as his right hand clamped down around her wrist, squeezing the gun free from her grip. The woman let out an enraged howl, momentarily surprising Mac with both her strength and ferocity as her free hand attempted to scratch at the former Navy SEAL's eyes.

"ENOUGH!"

Mac grasped Milla's throat with his left hand and the inside of her right thigh with his right hand and lifted her upward, slamming her body into the 767's ceiling, and then dropping her back onto the cabin floor where she remained unmoving.

"Tie her up, cover her mouth, and put her in one of the bathrooms."

Stasia had already picked up the handgun, and was looking it over.

"Basic SIG Sauer P229, nine round capacity, with seven rounds remaining."

Mac moved toward a window and opened it just enough to allow him to peer outside the plane. On the ground below, two armed men continued to refuel the plane, while some fifty yards behind them, a group of three more armed men were moving toward them, one man carrying what appeared to be at least two military assault rifles in his arms.

"Danika, where are you?"

The other female flight attendant stepped forward from inside the first class area, her panicked eyes looking down at the unconscious Milla as she was dragged into a bathroom by Walter.

"Danika, there will be some men coming onto the plane very soon. Keep them happy, ok? As for everyone else, we're gonna get you out of those zip ties, but I need you to remain in your seats. Don't move, don't say anything, just look down at your feet. Right now, we don't have the firepower to fight back. If they get even a hint of trouble, they'll come in here blasting and that will be that. Everyone understand?"

The heavy set man with the "American Badass" tattoo stood up.

"I'm not listening to a goddamn thing you have to say, asshole! You're gonna get us all killed! Untie us, and I say we all fight whoever tries to get on this plane! Don't ask me to sit in my seat like some idiot waiting to die!"

Mac knew they didn't have time for argument. The three Tunisian military men were likely at the bottom of the boarding steps, hopefully talking to the other two who were fueling the plane. Mac noted the man's young son was once again crying in his seat.

"Sir, if you don't shut up and sit down, your son will die in this plane. I need you, I need *everyone*, to listen to my directions. I don't have the time to explain right now, but believe me, this ain't my first rodeo. You're gonna have a chance to fight back, but we have to choose the right time, and this isn't it, not yet. Please sir, sit down."

American Badass looked at Mac, and then Stasia before glancing down at his crying son. A moment later he sat down in his seat while telling the boy to be quiet.

"They're coming up the boarding stairs!"

Danika hissed the warning as her eyes held Mac's for several seconds before she disappeared toward the front of the plane.

"Remember Danika, keep them happy, and try to keep them from coming back here."

Mac and Stasia moved back behind the food prep area curtain where Walter was already waiting. He motioned toward one of the bathrooms.

"I put her in there. She's still unconscious."

Mac nodded silently as he peered out from behind the curtain. The passengers were doing as they were told, sitting silently, not moving, and looking down.

The sound of Danika's laughter filtered to the back of the plane.

Good girl, she's flirting, distracting them.

Mac's praise was short lived as a short, uniformed man in his late 30's walked slowly into the primary passenger area of the plane. His dark eyes scanned the rows of seats, stopping to stare at each passenger before moving on to the next. In his hands he held an older, Soviet made AK-47 with the common 30 round magazine.

Stasia stood on the opposite side of the blue curtain, holding the SIG Sauer and looking more than ready to use it if need be.

More of Danika's forced laughter filled the 767 cabin. Mac detected a hint of nervousness in it, and hoped the woman could keep it together long enough to get the Tunisian soldiers back off the plane. The soldier who had entered the cabin turned his head at the sound of Danika laughing, and disappeared toward the front of the plane where he began barking orders that they were to return outside after leaving the weapons on the plane for the captain and his crew.

Mac let out the breath he wasn't aware he had been holding.

So far so good…

"Walter, is there anything in here that you can use to cut all the zip ties with?"

Walter turned and opened a drawer from which he withdrew a butter knife.

"This is all we got."

Mac looked down at the knife and then nodded.

"That'll be fine, Walter. Just have the passengers pull their hands apart as far as they can, and then you pull up with the knife. I need you to move as fast as you can on this, we probably only have a few minutes before we get some more visitors."

Walter's face took on a decidedly determined look as his eyes narrowed and his jaw set. He moved quickly past Mac and began to work the first of the passengers free from their bonds.

"Stasia, stay with the passengers and keep them calm and focused. We may need them ready to fight soon."

The Vatican Intelligence agent began to move out into the main cabin and then stopped to turn around and face Mac.

"Where are you going?"

Mac's eyes motioned toward the front of the plane.

"The cockpit - gonna try and send out a communication. Figured it was worth a try."

Stasia smiled as she held the SIG Sauer up next to her face.

"Tell you what, Mac, we get out of this alive and dinner's on me."

Mac leaned in so his own face was a mere inches from Stasia's, his voice a near whisper.

"Do I look like the kind of guy who lets a woman buy him dinner?"

Stasia moved her mouth close enough that her lips brushed the outside of Mac's right ear as she murmured her response.

"Do I look like the kind of girl who gives a shit?"

24.

Though he had always favored the American made AR-15 to the AK-47, Mac Walker was never so happy to see a pair of the Soviet made assault rifles lying just outside of the cockpit as he was that day. Those rifles provided them sixty rounds in which to defend themselves, a number that Mac felt provided, if not fair odds, at least the possibility to be able to fight back. Plus, there was the air marshal's weapon which Stasia still held. That was another seven rounds of firepower.

Shortly after picking up the rifles, Mac sat in the 767's cockpit with Walter, trying to decipher the plane's communications system while ignoring the body of the co-pilot which remained shoved in the right back corner of the narrow and low ceilinged confines of the cockpit space.

"That shouldn't be there. What is it?"

Mac's eyes followed to where Walter was pointing out a small, yellowish metallic box, similar in size to an old school lunch pale from his childhood, that sat to the far right of the cockpit panel. The back of the box was constructed of a clear plastic, inside of which Mac could see a series of thin wires, and thicker cables, as well as what appeared to be a sizeable battery. A single circular LED light no larger than the tip of an eraser was housed on the bottom half of the box and flashed green every few seconds.

"Is that a bomb?"

The panic in Walter's voice was clear. Mac shook his head.

"No, I don't think so. If I had to guess, I'd say it's some kind of electronic blocking device. I've seen something similar to this, though a much larger version, used to black out cell phone coverage for an area the size of a small village. I suppose this one would be large enough to keep everyone on the plane from being able to use their cell phones. If none of the passengers could get a call out, that would reinforce the belief by investigators that the flight suffered some kind of catastrophic occurrence, and give the hijackers more time to do whatever it is they intend to do with this plane – and all of us."

Walter separated the back of the box from the rest of its body by several inches, looking down at the myriad of wires attached to the batter device. He then looked up at Mac who then shrugged.

"Rip 'em out Walter. See if we can shut it off."

The flight attendant reached a thin fingered right hand into the opening and grasped onto several wires and then pulled. The LED light turned to a constant red color.

"Well you did something. Let me try my cell."

Before Mac could remove his Project Icon cell phone, Walter pointed outside.

"More of them coming this way."

Two more armed soldiers were making their way toward the 767, carrying a simple wooden box between them. Mac knew he had very little time to construct a plan, though despite that fact, he remained absolutely calm, focusing his energies not on panic, but a practical application of action and reaction that was the foundation of every great soldier throughout history.

"Walter, I want you to be the one to greet those two soldiers. You're wearing an airline uniform, so they'll assume you're part of the captain's flight crew. They won't know any better. Direct them to place that box in the cargo hold. Get their attention and hold it – all I need is a second or two."

Walter let out a slow sigh and then nodded back at Mac.

"Ok, I can do it."

The male flight attendant stood up and tucked his shirt into his pants, trying to look as professional as possible.

"You look fine, Walter. Like I said, into the cargo hold and then keep their attention for a second or two."

While Walter left the cockpit, Mac stayed back, hiding himself just behind the door. He could hear the soldiers making their way slowly up the boarding steps, complaining about how heavy the box was. Mac couldn't understand every word they spoke, but over the years, and countless missions, he had managed to pick up a bit of language from nearly every corner of the globe.

"Yes, come in. You can put that right inside here."

Mac smiled to himself, happy to hear Walter doing such a good job of sounding so at ease. Next came the sound of the cargo door being opened and the soldiers grunting as they shuffled the box just past where Mac stood hiding behind the cockpit door.

"The captain wants the box on the other end of the cargo hold over there."

Again Mac was impressed with Walter's clear thinking. The soldiers' attention would be on getting the box to the back of the cargo hold, and not on what was coming up behind them.

Mac Walker slipped silently into the cargo area, no more than ten feet from where the two Tunisian soldiers were still complaining over the weight of the box they had been ordered to deliver. He held one of the two AK-47s and was pointing it at the back of the soldier on the left, but knowing the last thing he wanted to be doing was opening fire. The sound would bring more soldiers, and put the passengers at risk of being slaughtered.

A high pitched, friendly whistle issued from Mac's lips as his body tensed, awaiting the moment to act.

The soldier on the right was the first to turn at the whistling sound, his face greeted by the crunching impact of the butt of the AK-47 rifle, the blow cracking open the man's skull and sending his body dropping like a wet sack of potatoes, along with his half of the cargo box he had been holding onto.

The second soldier cursed as the right side of the box fell toward the floor, and then his mouth opened wider to shout out his shock at seeing his comrade being attacked. Mac's movement was a blur of hands and arms that resulted in his left hand clamped over the remaining soldier's mouth while the thumb of Mac's right hand jabbed twice into the cartilage of the man's throat.

The soldier fell, gasping for breath that would not come, as Mac then grasped onto his head from behind and twisted it violently to the right, causing the soldier's chin to move well past his right shoulder. Walter flinched as he heard the surprisingly loud, and sickening pop of the man's neck being broken.

Mac Walker wasted no time looking over the results of his efforts, his own attention already focused on the contents within the just delivered box, and soon, Walter found himself doing the same.

"What are those things?"

Mac shook his head.

"Not sure exactly, but I'd guess a chemical, or maybe biological weapon of some sort. Nasty looking things that's for sure. Close it back up."

As Walter put the cover back onto the cargo box, Mac strode quickly back toward the cockpit to take another look outside. The portable fueling container had been removed from the plane, and there appeared to be no soldiers inside of the hanger. A single drop of dark red blood splattered onto the cockpit floor from the end of the AK-47 Mac held, a remnant of the blow to the first soldier's forehead.

That bit of blood gave Mac Walker an idea. He had no intention of remaining inside of this plane much longer, knowing that eventually, their recently won freedom would be discovered, and everyone's lives likely ending shortly after.

Mac moved back into the cargo hold where Walter was dragging the bodies of the soldiers behind the just delivered box containing the metallic cylinders.

The former Navy SEAL was already unbuttoning his shirt as he barked an order at the flight attendant.

"Walter – help me get out of these clothes. Hurry, we don't have much time."

Walter's brow catapulted upward as his mouth fell open. He did as he was told, running toward Mac Walker, his hands already working to pull Mac's pants off.

"Lucky you, Mr. Walker, if you ever need someone to rip your clothes off quickly, I'm your man."

25.

Stasia Wellington heard the commotion coming from the front of the plane and moved to investigate. What she found was Walter and Mac both in the cargo hold. Walter was on his knees in front of Mac attempting to pull his right foot free from his pant leg while Mac had a cell phone to his ear.

"Sorry, gentlemen, I didn't know you were on a date."

Mac looked over at Stasia and then down at Walter, and then wagged his finger at the Vatican Intelligence operative while shaking his head from side to side.

"No-no-no, this is *not* what it looks like. Just swapping some clothes out. We can't remain in here just waiting for something to happen. It's time to *make* something happen."

Stasia saw the military uniform on the floor just behind where Mac and Walter stood, and realized with no small amount of alarm, what the former Navy SEAL intended to do.

"You can't go out there by yourself Mac. There's too many of them, you'll be shot to pieces before you reach the bottom of the boarding steps."

Walter had grabbed a pair of the light olive colored Tunisian military pants and was helping Mac step into them while Mac attempted to dial a number on his cell phone.

"C'mon, Tilley take the damn call."

The attempt went to voice mail.

"Tilley, it's Mac. The plane was hijacked. We are currently sitting inside a makeshift hanger somewhere on the Tunisian coast. These people intend to bomb the Vatican using some kind of chemical or biological weapon. Alert Italian authorities, and pull the satellite data for this location. The shit's about to hit the fan here, and I'd be happy for whatever help you can send my way. Gonna do everything I can to keep this plane grounded. Walker out."

Mac Walker was fully dressed in the military uniform.

"Thanks for the help, Walter. Take the weapons from those two and keep one for yourself, and give the other one to the younger Black guy in the cabin – the one that was sitting across from me. He seems to be keeping his wits about him."

Walter moved to leave, but then stopped as Stasia posed a question.

"Did you turn the transponder back on? I assume the captain shut it off to allow the plane to fly without being easily tracked. If you turned it back on, they'll pick up the signal within minutes."

Mac felt like an idiot, realizing he hadn't thought to do that earlier.

"Walter, can you take care of it?"

The flight attendant nodded and then disappeared into the cockpit holding an AK-47 in each of his hands.
"Normally I wouldn't have missed something like that. Thanks for pointing it out."

Stasia gave her shoulders a slight shrug and then placed a hand on each of Mac Walker's shoulders.

"So how's this going to end for us, Mr. Walker? You really think we can keep all of these people safe? How many guns are out there waiting for us?"

Mac shook his head momentarily forgetting about what he knew was awaiting him outside the plane. Instead, he simply wanted to enjoy looking into Stasia's eyes, and wondering if they would be given the opportunity to get to know each other better.

"Remember, you said you'd buy me dinner after we're done here."

Stasia placed her right hand behind Mac's head and pulled him toward her, kissing him gently on the left cheek.

"I hope to be able to keep that promise Mr. Walker, so don't go getting yourself killed."

Mac began to pull away, and then realized Stasia was right – he was likely to die soon. He had just thirty rounds of ammunition against multiple armed men outside. Even for one as well trained and experienced as him, the odds were not proving kind.

That meant a kiss on the cheek simply wouldn't do.

Mac's face moved back toward Stasia's as his right arm encircled the small of her back and pulled her aggressively against his body, his mouth pressing into hers. She welcomed the embrace, matching Mac's hungry intensity with ample amounts of her own.

It was an all too brief moment, a mere few seconds, but it left Stasia breathing heavily and looking up at Mac with unrefined lust.

"Don't you dare die out there, Mac Walker. There's going to be much more than a dinner waiting for you after this."

Mac looked Stasia up and down and then nodded, his eyes gleaming with the possibility of things to come.

"Alright then, looks like I got something to live for."

Thousands of miles away, at the same time Mac Walker was embracing Stasia Wellington, Ray Tilley stepped out of the shower and saw his Project Icon cell phone indicating a call had recently come in. He stood with a towel wrapped around his midsection and held the phone up and then felt a creeping, stunned numbness overtake his body.

The call had come from Mac Walker.

The son-of-a-bitch was alive!

Tilley realized his hand was shaking slightly as he held the phone to his ear to listen to the message.

Tilley, it's Mac. The plane was hijacked. We are currently sitting inside a makeshift hanger somewhere on the Tunisian coast. These people intend to bomb the Vatican using some kind of chemical or biological weapon. Alert Italian authorities, and pull the satellite data for this location. The shit's about to hit the fan here, and I'd be happy for whatever help you can send my way. Gonna do everything I can to keep this plane grounded. Walker out.

Tilley replayed the message twice, memorizing every word. Then he called Stephen Mardian, who picked up on the second ring.

"Mardian, I just received a message from Walker. The plane is being held in Tunisia, hidden inside a hanger. He confirmed the attack on Rome. The hijackers have a chemical or biological weapon. Sounds like he's about to take them on himself. Alert the general and see if we can scramble some fighters out of Sigonella. Find out if we have any CIA in the area, anything or anyone that can provide assistance."

Stephen Mardian's response was to push Tilley for clarification.

"Tunisia? What the hell would they be doing there? Are you certain it was Walker?"

Ray Tilley fought the urge to throw the phone against the wall, knowing every minute wasted put Mac Walker and the passengers at greater risk.

"The call came from his phone. It was his voice so yeah, I'm sure it was Walker. We don't have time to play what if, Mardian. Make the call to the general now. Those people in that plane need our help."

"Hold up Ray, I got another call coming in. It's the general."

Tilley stood shivering in his bathroom, each second of silence feeling like an eternity. Nearly three minutes passed before Mardian's voice continued.

"Pentagon reported a signal from the plane was received no more than ten minutes ago. Someone must have turned the transponder on. They've tracked the location. It's sitting on an uninhabited island about five miles off the Tunisian coast. We have a carrier from the Sixth Fleet about four hundred miles away. They're scrambling a pair of F-14s to the island with an ETA of no more than thirty minutes. No idea yet on how long it will take on the ground support to arrive."

"Has there been any official communications between our government and the Tunisians?"

Though he couldn't see him, Tilley knew Mardian was shaking his head.

"Not that I'm aware of. Our State Department is slow to react on this so far. As of now, it's strictly a Pentagon matter."

Ray Tilley lifted his head toward the ceiling as he closed his eyes and inhaled and then exhaled slowly while still keeping the cell phone to his ear.

"Looks like you were right about this Mac Walker, Ray. He's a fighter."
Tilley already knew that of course. He just hoped for Mac and the passengers of Atlantis Flight 444, it would prove enough to keep them all alive until help arrived.

26.

Father Victor Barnes ran down one of the many marble tiled corridors of the Vatican, having just received a phone message from Ray Tilley, a message Tilley initiated that was a direct violation of his own superior's orders. Mac Walker was alive, which meant Stasia was likely alive as well. The plane was somewhere along the Tunisian coast, being prepped for an attack on the Vatican – likely within the hour.

"Cardinal! I need to have a word with you – NOW!"

Cardinal Copilli turned around to face Father Barnes while at the same time, motioning to the two young male robed assistants to go on without him.

The cardinal's face betrayed his annoyance at seeing the priest moving toward him at such a deliberate pace.

"Running inside the Vatican, Father? What could possibly be so important for you to draw such unwanted attention to yourself?"

Father Barnes stood heaving in front of the cardinal, gasping to catch his breath.

"The plane, there's a signal. It's in Tunisia, just like I told you. I have a source in Washington D.C. who confirmed it. Mac Walker left him a message. The passengers were ok, but the plane was hijacked, and it's to be used as a weapon for an attack on the Vatican. My source believes the attack is imminent. Did you contact the president, the Italian military?"

Cardinal Copilli glanced behind the priest to see if anyone else was nearby. Satisfied they stood alone in the massive Vatican hallway, he took a step toward Father Barnes, his voice a hushed yet urgent whisper.

"Have you spoken to anyone else about this, Father?"

Father Barnes shook his head, somewhat confused by the question.

"No…I spoke with my D.C. source and then made my way directly to you, why?"

The cardinal placed his right hand on the priest's well muscled shoulder and squeezed it lightly.

"I don't wish to unnecessarily panic anyone. I will contact the office of the Holy Father personally as soon as I return to my study and inform them of what you just told me. Was there any word on Stasia Wellington? Is she ok?"

Father Barnes's confusion increased, as well as his already considerable suspicion regarding what was motivating Cardinal Copilli's actions throughout this crisis.

"I assume she's ok, yes. And I imagine she will be helping to keep all of the passengers alive and well until help can arrive."

A very brief, almost undetectable flash of disappointment crossed over the cardinal's face. He quickly recovered though, and smiled up at the priest.

"That is very good then. Lord willing, everyone will be safe and this terrible attempt will be thwarted, and those responsible will be punished. Now if you will excuse me, I am off to raise the alarm. Oh, and good work, Father. Well done."

As Father Barnes watched the quickly departing cardinal scurry off to his office, the priest realized his papal superior had avoided giving any indication of whether or not he had already notified Italian authorities of the threat, as he had promised earlier to do.

What is that rat faced little bastard up to?
At the same time as Father Barnes posed that question to himself, Mac Walker was addressing the passengers of Atlantis Flight 444.

"Right now, the safest place for all of you is inside this aircraft. The hijackers won't harm this plane if they believe there's a chance they can still use it as a weapon. They'll try and take it back first, and that's where I come in. I'm gonna be out there holding them off, buying us some time, until U.S. military arrive, or the Italians or whatever other friendly force gets here first. Until then though, it's us against them, and that means we need to stick together, and be prepared for anything."

"Why the hell do you get to decide how we defend ourselves? Why do you get a gun, and not me?"

It was the tattooed father once again placing himself as a most determined pain in Mac Walker's ass. Though his first inclination was to tell the asshole to shut his mouth, Mac decided a change in tone might illicit a more favorable result.

"Who I am isn't important right now, sir. The fact I might be your single best hope of keeping you and your boy alive, is all that matters. I need your help though – we all do. Like I said, this is gonna take everyone working together. What's your name?"

The man's eyes narrowed, uncertain if Mac was mocking him or being sincere. He glanced to the other passengers on his left and then his right, before finally responding.

"Lenny…Lenny Rorke. This is my son Lenny Jr."

Mac offered up a half smile, appreciating the avoidance of yet another confrontation with the Lenny.

"Nice to know your name, Mr. Rorke. I'm sorry about earlier, that was…that was me being me. I'm not always the most patient of people, especially when I think the safety of others is at risk."

Lenny straightened his shoulders, more grateful of Mac's apology than Mac thought he would be. The former Navy SEAL was not a father, and did not understand that for a man to be seen as weak in front of his son would make the alleged source of that shame a father's number one enemy.

"No problem, man. Just tell me how we can help. I'm not about to sit on my ass waiting for the hijackers to come in here shooting."

Mac looked around at all the passengers sitting in the 767. Some were young, many were older. Most were American, returning home, like Mac, from vacationing in Paris. Some were French, travelling to the United States, while others were from other nations, visiting family in the States, or just hoping to see America for the first time.

They were all scared, though Mac Walker was impressed with how well they continued to maintain a surprising degree of calm given the circumstances. This included Eldra Peabody, who still sat in her seat, her warm eyes looking back at Mac with a mixture of pride and affection.

"I'll be the first line of defense. The woman standing next to me, and the young man just behind me, will be the second line of defense. They will guard the entrance. If they go down, it's up to all of you to keep this plane from taking off. Every one of you must do whatever it takes, to prevent that from happening, because if this plan gets back in the air, it could be used to kill thousands of people, and we can't let that happen. We *won't* let that happen."

The passengers looked at both Stasia and Walter, and then their eyes returned to Mac Walker as he stood there calmly holding an AK-47 over his left shoulder as if he were about to embark on a leisurely Sunday stroll. They knew the risk Mac was about to take – knew it likely meant his death. He was but one man against many.

Then again, they didn't really know Mac Walker.

27.

"I believe the weapon should be securely in place on the plane, Captain. The craft has been refueled, and you are ready to depart, may Allah protect us and bless the justice you bring to the infidels of the Catholic Satan."

Captain Rogers was nervous, his eyes scanning the distance between the colonel's office structure, and the hangar. He could see the outline of the boarding steps and noted to himself how the two soldiers who were to deliver the chemical canisters had yet to return.

"Where are your soldiers, Colonel? The ones who carried the canisters onto the plane?"

Colonel Mabazza waved a dismissive hand toward the captain, shaking his head and chuckling.

"Captain, you must learn to relax! All is well! All is well! My men are the very best. Well trained and highly professional! They likely took a moment to ensure the passengers remain in their seats, like perfect little lambs awaiting their slaughter. Ok? Please, allow me a toast in honor of this great occasion of which you are its primary component!"

Captain Roger's jaw set as he glared at the colonel. The man claimed to be a devoted Muslim, and yet, here he sat pouring himself alcohol.

"I do not drink, Colonel. *As you know*, the Koran forbids it, and my soul must be in a state of purity if I am to ascend to paradise later this day."

Colonel Mabazza's eyes flashed indignation at the captain's implied challenge, though the smile remained on his lean, smooth shaven face. For the colonel, the fanatics were useful tools, easily motivated, but entirely expendable. Just like the airline pilot who now sat before him.

No worries, let the idiot make his religious speech. He will be dead and gone soon enough, but my journey to greater power will continue.

"Of course, Captain, how rude of me to suggest otherwise. Ah, look there! The soldiers are returning now."

Captain Rogers turned to confirm what the colonel saw. A moment of relief washed over him as his own eyes took on the form of one of the uniformed Tunisian soldiers walking slowly back down the boarding steps.

The relief evaporated as he realized the other soldier was missing, his paranoia at something going wrong once again gripping him.

"Where is second soldier, Colonel? Why is only one of them returning?"

Colonel Mabazza followed the captain's gaze toward the makeshift island hangar. He could see one of his uniformed soldiers nearing the bottom of the boarding steps, though his face was hidden within the shadows of the hangar's interior. Just outside the hangar, another soldier was making his way inside the hangar as well.

"No worries, Captain, see? All appears to be fine."

A loud, clapping noise reverberated across the beach as the colonel watched the soldier who had been walking toward the boarding steps suddenly fall to the ground, where he remained unmoving.

Captain Rogers stood up snarling back at the colonel.

"You wretched dog! What is this? We are under attack by one of your own men!"

Colonel Mabazza ignored the captain's outrage, instead ordering four of his men to take positions just outside the hangar. Flight 444's hijacking air marshal, Reyos Huskich, holding an AK-47, had already made his way to Captain Roger's side.

"It's the army boy, has to be. The idiots delivered to him the very weapons he will now be using against us!"

The captain's lips pulled back from his teeth as he watched the colonel's men slowly encircle the hangar. With the just slain Tunisian soldier, and the two other soldiers who had been sent to deliver the weapon onto the plane also likely dead, Captain Rogers realized their opponent was proving far more capable than Huskich's derisive "army boy" designation implied.

Whoever that man standing inside the hangar was, he clearly knew his way around the business of killing.

Another two shots were fired from within the hangar, causing the Tunisian soldiers to scramble for cover, their cries of alarm drowning out the echoes of earlier gunfire.

The air marshal growled his disgust.

"Cowards, they look as if they've never been shot at!"

Captain Rogers grunted his agreement and then turned to his fellow terrorist.

"Can you circle the structure, kill him from behind?"

Reyos Huskich nodded once and then began making his way to the other side of the hangar, circling wide to avoid being seen doing so. Captain Rogers watched Huskich's progress as the four Tunisian soldiers fired multiple rounds into the hangar and then waited for a response. When none came, one of the soldiers began pumping his fist and declared they had killed the traitor.

This celebration was cut short by a single gunshot from the hangar, and then the side of the soldier's head detonating as Mac Walker's Ak-47 tore through the Tunisian's skull. The three remaining soldiers began firing their weapons in a mixture of rage and panic, still not believing anyone could be so accurate with a weapon noted for quantity of rounds fired, not quality.

The captain turned toward the water as he heard the sound of a marine engine roaring to life. On one of the two boats that had brought the Tunisians from the naval vessel to the island, was Colonel Mabazza and another of his soldiers, clearly intending to escape the island and the deadly chaos that now threatened to overtake it.

"Cowardly pig! You run away? Allah will damn you to hell!"

The colonel waved back at the captain as the boat plunged into the water and raced away, the scream of its engine indicating it was being pushed to its limits in order to safely return Colonel Mabazza back to the awaiting Tunisian military vessel.

Captain Rogers turned back to once again face the hangar, realizing only three armed Tunisian soldiers remained, as well as himself and Reyos Huskich. Five armed men left to face one.

Surely that would be enough.

As the rogue airline captain who hoped to decimate the Vatican stood pondering the odds of the hijackers taking back the plane, Mac Walker lay on his belly inside of the hangar, watching the three Tunisian soldiers attempting to inch their way closer toward him. The soldiers appeared uncertain, and likely far more afraid for their own lives than Mac was of losing his.

In fact, these were the moments of life and death wherein Mac Walker seemed to find himself most at peace. His mind became entirely focused on the task directly in front of him, with no distractions from the myriad of secondary concerns that life too often presented. Free from boredom, or transient obligation, there was only the here, and the now, to live, or to die, to kill, or be killed.

Such risk was the essence of Mac Walker, making up who he truly was, and likely who he would always be.

Multiple other rounds were fired into the hangar, missing well above Mac's prone body. The former Navy SEAL silently rolled several feet to his left, and then scrambled to the far wall on the right at the hangar's main opening. He could see one of the Tunisian soldiers attempting to move into the hangar from the left side, the soldier's body plastered against the outside wall as he shuffled closer.

Mac silently lifted the AK-47 upward and peered through its sight, locking in on the soldier's position no more than forty yards from where Mac crouched in the shadows of the hangar's interior.

Another single shot and the soldier fell backward, a bullet leaving a massive gash in his neck just below the chin. It took less than twenty seconds for him to bleed out, his body twitching as the last remnants of life left the soldier's body.

Mac Walker knew that left two soldiers just outside the hangar, and then the possibility of more to arrive from the ship that sat five hundred yards offshore. He had heard the sounds of a departing boat, and knew it likely meant someone had left in order to bring back reinforcements.

Nothing could be done about that though. For now he would simply focus on the two other soldiers who yet remained.

Mac didn't feel the aluminum fragment as it imbedded into the lower back portion of his skull, though the impact pushed him down onto the ground where he found himself looking up at the high ceiling above him and wondering what had just happened as his right hand scrambled to grip the AK-47 that lay next to him.

The sound of gunfire seemed to be coming from a great distance, even as Mac Walker knew it was in fact just outside the wall that separated him from the Tunisian soldiers. He could see small holes of daylight streaming above him, shooting across the hangar and lighting up the outline of the silent 767 that sat behind him like some great hibernating metallic beast inside the bowels of a cave.

Shot in the head. I've been shot in the head. Got to move. Get up. Get up. They're coming in. Protect the passengers. Move your ass Walker! Get up!

An unrelenting ringing noise filled Mac's ears as he pushed himself onto his knees, nearly overcome by nausea as he did so. He could feel a thick wetness on the back of his neck, and knew it was his own blood.

Get up!

Somehow, Mac Walker found himself standing, the AK-47 cradled in his arms as his body lurched to the left and then the right. He could see the shadowy outlines of both the remaining Tunisian soldiers making their way into the hangar.

Come and get some assholes…

28.

Stasia peered out from one of the left side cockpit windows, trying to see if Mac was ok. She heard the gunfire, and thought she saw him fall. Behind her, in the main cabin, some of the passengers cried out as each shot was fired from outside. Walter stood behind her, holding an assault rifle, his eyes wide, and his hands trembling slightly.

The Vatican Intelligence agent inhaled sharply as she watched Mac's form rise from the packed earth ground, clearly wobbly, but otherwise intact. He was fighting on.

"Stasia, there's someone coming from the other side of the hangar. Look."

Walter was pointing toward one of the left side windows. He was right, a shadowy form moved slowly but deliberately toward Mac's position.

He'll be trapped, pinned down, shot at from both sides.

Stasia Wellington turned to Walter. The flight attendant already knew what she intended, and was shaking his head in protest.

"You're supposed to stay here, Stasia – protect the entrance. If Mac dies, you're the next line of defense."

Walter was right of course, those were the instructions Mac had left her with. That didn't mean she intended to follow them though, especially when it meant watching Mac shot to pieces when she could have done something to prevent it.

"That's going to be your job, Walter. If something happens out there, if I can't make it back, you get all the passengers to the very back of the plane and you hold this position here for as long as you can, ok?"

Walter continued to protest, his panic compounded by the idea of being the one responsible for keeping others alive.

"I'm not a soldier, I don't know how---"

Stasia cut him off.

"You'd be surprised what any of us are capable of when we have to be Walter. You WILL hold this position. Any of those soldiers try to make their way inside, you shoot the bastards. Don't waste ammo though, make every shot count. You sent out a distress call, right?"

The flight attendant nodded.

"Yeah, about ten minutes ago."

Stasia smiled.

"Good, then it's just a waiting game for us. Help is coming, Walter so we just need to buy a little more time. See you soon."

And with those words, Stasia Wellington opened the cockpit boarding door and made her way quickly down the steps, crouching low and moving with the kind of stealth a cat would have envied. At the bottom of the steps she stopped, looking first to Mac's position some fifty yards north of her, and then the last noted location of the figure moving from the back of the hangar, which was nearly a hundred yards south.

She could hear Mac's feet shuffling as he held himself up against a wall. He hadn't noticed Stasia's descent, and had no idea she was watching him. From her position just behind the boarding steps, she could make out one of the two Tunisian soldiers ducking low, trying to gain access into the hangar.

Stasia moved to the other side of the 767's landing gear, hoping to locate the man attempting to sneak up behind Mac. She stood unmoving, holding her breath as her eyes peered into the structure's dimly lit interior.

There he is – Huskich.

The air marshal was no more than sixty yards in front of Stasia, moving along a wall as he continued to creep up behind Mac Walker. The Vatican Intelligence operative raised her weapon and took aim, confident in the imminent kill shot.

Several rounds of gunfire exploded to her left, coming from the hangar entrance. The Tunisian soldier's were making their move, with one providing cover while the other scrambled inside.

When Stasia's vision returned to where Reyos Huskich had been standing just a moment earlier, she found him gone.

Shit.

More gunfire sounded, followed by a high pitched howl of pain. Stasia couldn't tell if the sound came from Mac, or one of the Tunisian soldiers.

Where is he?

There was more gunfire, another scream, and then silence, with still no sign of the hijacking air marshal.

The outline of Mac Walker could be seen leaning against a wall, his left hand reaching out to steady himself while his right hand was struggling with something on the AK-47. Stasia wanted to yell out to Mac, to warn him, but knew doing so would reveal her own position and eliminate the advantage of surprise against Huskich.

Then she saw the air marshal no more than forty feet to Mac's right, pointing his own assault rifle at Mac's head. From that distance Stasia knew he wouldn't miss.

She raised her weapon and fired several rounds without regard to aim, hoping to get lucky, but at the very least, buying Mac some time to move. Mac Walker did indeed react quickly, but not away from Huskich, as Stasia thought he would, but rather directly toward him, launching his body onto the stunned air marshal who had fallen to the ground as several rounds ripped through the air no more than a few feet above him.

The sound of the struggle between Mac and Reyos Huskich echoed throughout the hangar as Stasia moved quickly toward the two men with her weapon at the ready. She couldn't fire though, as Mac and Huskich rolled across the hard packed earth, fighting to overcome the other, both men's rifles laying on the ground several paces away from them.

Stasia could see Mac was weakening, his struggle quickly transforming from one of attack, to one of desperate survival. She ran to where Reyos Huskich sat atop the former Navy SEAL, with both of his powerful hands clamped around Mac's neck, choking the life from him. It was then she saw the wound at the back of Mac's head, wondering to herself how he had managed to continue fighting at all.

"Let him go you prick…NOW."

Huskich looked up at Stasia and snarled his rebuke, his eyes lit with fanatical fire.

"No woman will ever order me. Not in this life. That plane is ours. It is Allah's will!"

Mac's face was turning a deep red as his eyes rolled into his skull, a low whistling of air issuing from his half open mouth.

Stasia knew there was no reasoning with madness. The only option was to kill it.

Gunfire echoed once again from inside the hangar, but it was not from Stasia's weapon, but rather from someone behind her. She felt the hot sting of a bullet scorching across her upper right shoulder, and knew she had been shot. The wound provided all the distraction Reyos Huskich needed as he lunged upward to grasp onto Stasia's AK-47, attempting to rip it from her hands.

The Vatican Intelligence operative recovered from the shock of being shot nearly as soon as it happened, twisting her body under Huskich's outreached arms and using her right leg to brace itself behind the air pilot's legs, allowing her to send the much heavier opponent crashing onto the ground.

Huskich maintained his grip on Stasia's weapon though, which caused her to fall as well. The air marshal used his own momentum to roll on top of her, his right fist smashing into the side of her head. The blow caused Stasia's vision to momentarily fade out, as her considerable and instinctive desire for self preservation screamed that she remain conscious.

The air marshal attempted another punch to her face, but Stasia had managed to free her right arm, ignoring the pain of her bullet wound, and sending the bottom half of her palm crashing upward into Huskich's chin, snapping the man's head back. Then her right leg slid upward toward her chest, allowing the inside of her right knee to curl around the air marshal's neck. The strength of that leg proved too much for Reyos Huskich as his upper body was pushed violently into the dirt with enough force it left him gasping for breath.

Stasia Wellington knew if she were to survive this encounter, hesitation was not an option. As the air marshal attempted to push himself up from a crouching position, his lungs still crying out for air, the bottom of Stasia's right foot impacted the bridge of Huskich's nose, tearing cartilage, and sending a torrent of blood pouring down over his mouth and chin.

The air marshal's eyes had been overtaken by the realization he was truly in trouble, unbelieving it could be happening at the hands of a woman.

Stasia saw that realization in Reyos Huskich, and it brought her pleasure, but not so much pleasure as when her left foot smashed into the right side of the air marshal's jaw, choking him on three of his own dislodged teeth, and then the satisfying crunch of the hijacker's throat being utterly destroyed by the heel of her right foot as it slammed down onto the vulnerable cartilage, leaving Huskich a soon to be dead, quivering mass of broken flesh.

Guess you should have followed a woman's orders after all you pig.

29.

Mac Walker watched Stasia dispense of Huskich through the blurred haze of eyes still struggling to focus after his head injury. He marveled at how fast she moved, and the way in which she was able to leverage Huskich's bulk against him.

The woman knew how to fight.

There was gunfire coming from somewhere else in the hangar.

In the space of just a few seconds, Mac fought to focus his thoughts. He was certain someone had fired toward Stasia just moments earlier, which meant they were likely preparing to do so again.

Mac could smell the dark, musky odor of dirt, mixing with the more acrid, burnt paper stench of recent gunfire. Stasia was moving toward him, crouching low in the gloom, trying to present a smaller target to whoever remained inside the hangar. She knelt next to Mac and gently pushed his head forward to examine the wound.

"Oh my, you got yourself quite a bit of metal lodged in this hard head of yours, Mr. Walker."

Stasia was looking down at an inch long piece of shrapnel from the hangar wall that had been blasted apart from the Tunisian soldiers' gunfire outside and then imbedded into the bone of Mac Walker's skull. A slightly larger piece would likely have found itself all the way into Mac's brain.

"That's ok, at least it's not something I use much."

Stasia smiled at Mac's attempt at humor, while at the same time scanning the area for any sign of where the most recent round of gunfire had originated from.

"Help me back up. We're still not alone in here."

Leaning heavily on Stasia's shoulder, Mac Walker once again stood upright, ignoring his body's demand he lay back down.

"You're shot."

Stasia had forgotten about the bullet wound to her right shoulder, but Mac's reminder pushed the pain back to the forefront of her awareness.

"Thanks, it felt fine until you mentioned it."

Mac was looking at the entry wound, and then located the exit wound. Satisfied it was little more than a flesh wound, he offered the Vatican Intelligence operative a grin.

"Next time – duck."

Raucous gunfire ripped through the hangar, though its location was well removed from where Mac and Stasia stood. They both looked toward the 767, hearing the collective screams of passengers, followed by yet more blasts from at least two AK-47s.

"Oh my god."

Both Stasia and Mac ran toward the boarding steps, though Stasia was a few steps quicker as Mac struggled to overcome the urge to pass out. Before she reached the bottom of the steps, the primary boarding door opened as a body fell backwards, tumbling end over end before coming to a stop halfway down the steps, its head twisted like some grotesque mannequin, leaving its face staring blankly behind its shoulders.

"Who is it?"

Mac called up to Stasia, who had descended the steps two at time and then stopped to look down at the bullet riddled body with the broken neck.

"The captain."

Mac Walker forced himself up toward Stasia, taking each step carefully as he fought to keep the world from spinning into darkness around him.

The lifeless form of Captain Rogers stared back at Mac through unblinking eyes, an assault rifle still clenched in his right hand.

"Help! He's bleeding! We need help!"

The plea for help came from inside the plane. Stasia was once again on the move, with Mac struggling to keep up. He could hear people crying, while others were attempting to comfort them.

Just inside the 767's entrance, adjacent to the cockpit door, was Walter. He sat on the floor with his back against a wall, his legs splayed out in front of him. Both of his hands covered the blood drenched front of his Atlantis Airlines shirt. Mac could see the blood oozing out with each beat of Walter's heart. He had been shot at least a half dozen times.

Walter looked up at both Stasia and Mac and gave a weak half shrug of his shoulders. His eyes said far more than the shrug – confident there was to be no more tomorrows.

Mac Walker knew that look all too well, having seen it more times than he cared to recall in the eyes of enemies and comrades alike. Within that knowing was the understanding that his own inevitable end would come to pass as well, and he hoped to meet that end as bravely and selflessly as Walter was doing.

Eldra moved from the main cabin toward Walter and leaned down to cradle his head in her arms, and then whispered something into his ear. Mac watched as Walter smiled and mumbled a thank you. The blood from his wounds continued to push outward between his fingers for a few more seconds, and then the flow slowed, and finally, stopped.

Walter Hill was dead.

Eldra's eyes glistened with tears as she looked up at Stasia and Mac, the old woman's lower lip trembling as her right hand continued to gently stroke Walter's hair.

"He was so brave. We knew someone was coming, trying to get in, and he told us to lie down and be still, and then...then the gunfire. It was so loud, so terrible. I know it was no more than a second or two, but it felt like forever, that awful-awful sound. He put himself between that killer and all of us. This poor, beautiful young man did that for people he didn't even know. I just..."

Eldra's words were cut off by her own muffled sobs.

Stasia lifted her head upward, and then turned around to look down the boarding steps.

"You hear that?"

Mac closed his eyes and then confirmed what Stasia indicated – the unmistakable, growling roar of two F-14s passing overhead.

"Sounds like the cavalry has finally arrived."

After uttering those words, and hoping the safety of the passengers was in fact secured, Mac Walker finally relented to the demands of his wounded head.

He passed out.

30.

Stephen Mardian wanted the meeting to be over.

"Thank you for taking the time to conduct this informal hearing with us Mr. Walker. We'll let you know if we need any further information from you."

Mac had been sitting across a Pentagon conference room table from Stephen Mardian, Ray Tilley, and General Tinny, for the last two hours. It had been nine days since the firefight inside of the makeshift island hangar off the Tunisian coast. Three of those days were spent recovering aboard a U.S. naval vessel following the removal of the shrapnel from the back of his head, and the five days after that sitting inside a D.C. hotel room awaiting further instructions from Tilley.

"What happened to Colonel Mabazza?"

General Tinny's annoyance was clearly conveyed by his fleshy frown and exaggerated clearing of his throat.

"The response to this incident in ongoing and doesn't concern you, Mr. Walker. The fewer questions you ask, the more appreciative of your cooperation we will be. Understood?"

Mac Walker leaned back in his chair while folding his arms across his chest, taking a moment to look each of the three men in the eyes before continuing. Ray Tilley had told him just a few days ago of the Tunisian colonel's involvement in the hijacking, but as of yet, none of that information had made its way to the media, and Mac wanted to know why.

"I would like to think your appreciation would include telling me the truth, General."

Mac watched as Mardian glanced at Tilley, his look a "keep your boy in line" order.

General Tinny's frown intensified as his nostrils flared.

"I haven't lied to you, Mr. Walker if that is what you're suggesting."

Mac shook his head. Few things in this world were as pathetic, or offensive, as a politician dressed in soldier's clothes. General Tinny was clearly a cover my ass politician of the worst kind.

"Well you sure as hell haven't told me the truth. Where are the media reports regarding the Tunisian government's involvement? What about the plot to attack the Vatican? Why isn't that being disseminated? Where is the other flight attendant, Danika? We're almost two weeks from when Atlantis Flight 444 was hijacked, and all I'm hearing are stories about mechanical difficulties, miscommunication between the flight crew and the airlines, and a possible emergency landing that left some people dead. Was that you who cooked up that plate of bullshit, General?"

Stephen Mardian leaned forward, his perfectly manicured hands gently folding into each other.

"Actually, that would be me who came up with that, Mr. Walker – at least partly. The surviving members of the flight crew, as would be expected, are being detained, and at least one of them, the Danika you mention, is cooperating with various agencies. As you should know by now, there are certain things we must do to protect the interests of the country and its people. This is one of those times. A lie that potentially saves lives, is an honorable thing. You may not like it, but what you like or don't like, means nothing to me, or the people I answer to. The sooner you understand that, the sooner you come to terms with your own clearly inflated sense of self importance, the more productive a relationship you can have with Project Icon."

Mac Walker could feel his anger quickly rising within him, threatening to overtake the need to remain calm. How he despised these D.C. hacks and their never ending schemes and power plays amongst themselves.

"With all due respect, Mr. Mardian, I don't give one little shit about your definition of honor, I just want to know why we ain't going after that Tunisian son-of-a-bitch who tried to see a planeload of chemical weapons dumped all over Rome? At the very least shouldn't we be sending a message to every other asshole in the world we ain't taking this shit no more? Wasn't that supposed to be the lesson of 9-11?"

General Tinny shook his head as he smirked back at Mac Walker.

"It's a little more complicated than that, Walker. I appreciate what you did helping to save those passengers, and keeping that plane from taking off, but you need to understand, there's more to this than just that plane, and the people you saved – a lot more. The world is changing, and we need to make certain to protect ourselves, and our interests, in the midst of that change."

Ray Tilley tapped the table lightly with the tips of his right hand fingers, trying to intervene before Mac's increasingly agitated opinion of the general and Stephen Mardian blew up right in front of them.

"How about you give Mr. Walker and myself a little time alone gentleman? I'd like to finalize our offer of having him join Project Icon."

General Tinny opened his mouth to say something, but was cut off by Mardian's raised right hand.

"That would be fine Ray, let us know how it goes. As for you Mr. Walker, I do hope to have you working for us. Clearly, you bring the kind of talents that could be put to very good use, and despite what you may be feeling now, we really are the good guys."

The general stood up while glaring down at the still seated Mac Walker, and then left the conference room without saying a word. Stephen Mardian offered a slight smile, adjusted his custom made, dark red tie, and then followed behind the general, leaving Mac and Tilley by themselves at the table.

"Mac, I know you're pissed, but people like that are a necessary evil. Without them, there is no Project Icon. They provide the funding, the diplomatic protections, identifications, all the peripheral tools we need to do what we do. You don't need to worry about them though – that's what I'm for. Once you're in the field, you don't have anyone to answer to but yourself. Tinny doesn't like you, says you don't play well with others, but you remember Francesca Porter with the Senate Intelligence Committee? She gave you an enthusiastic green light, told Mardian personally she thinks you would be an incredibly valuable asset to us."

Mac's arms were still folded across his chest as he looked back at Ray Tilley.

"What happened to Stasia Wellington? Is she ok?"

Tilley nodded, sensing Mac's concern for the Vatican Intelligence operative was both genuine, and well beyond a mere passing interest.

"As far as I know, yes. I'm certain they've debriefed her just as we did you, and from there, I suppose she's back to work doing whatever she was doing before. Believe me, we've tried to figure out what that is, but the Vatican is not terribly forthcoming about such information. I take it she impressed you?"

Mac grinned to himself as he recalled Stasia's toughness and considerable combat abilities.

"Yeah – she did."

Ray Tilley paused for a moment, and then proceeded with his offer to Mac Walker.

"So are you in, Mac? Can I put you down as operational for Project Icon? My plan is to assemble you a team, just a few other high quality operatives like yourself, and then some get in get out assignments, tough, dangerous - but lucrative. I need to know now though if you're in, or out."

Mac closed his eyes and rolled his head slowly from side to side, noting the twinge of pain that still existed where the shrapnel fragment was recently removed from the back of his skull.

When his eyes reopened, he looked across the conference room table at a clearly hopeful Ray Tilley, and nodded slowly.

"Yeah, I'm in."

Shortly after telling Ray Tilley he would join up with Project Icon, Mac Walker found himself outside in one of the many expansive Pentagon parking areas looking back at the all too familiar and shapely form of Stasia Wellington.

She stood next to a rented white four door sedan, wearing a form fitting dark blue dress and matching heels, her thick, dark hair falling over her shoulders in light curls. She flashed an enthusiastic smile at Mac as he walked toward her.

"You're not going to faint on me again are you?"

Mac stopped in front of Stasia and looked her up and down, admiring the view she was happily offering him.

"No ma'am, feeling much better now. Maybe even a hundred percent. You think you can handle a hundred percent Stasia?"

Stasia feigned outrage, as her lips pursed and she shook her head at Mac.

"Are you being crude, Mr. Walker?"

Mac leaned in close enough that his left cheek brushed up against Stasia's right cheek.

"Absolutely, Ms. Wellington."

Stasia turned her head slightly and playfully bit down on Mac's ear lobe.

"Good, I'm in the mood for some crude."

Mac leaned back, and shook a finger in front of Stasia's face.

"Not so fast. You promised me a dinner, remember? I won't be any good to you on an empty stomach."

Stasia's right hand reached down and gently squeezed Mac's crotch as she leaned in to whisper her response.

"It's not your stomach I'm interested in."

Mac issued a low, hungry growl as he inhaled the scent of Stasia's skin in that delicious space where neck met shoulder.

"Mmmmm, maybe I can skip a meal or two, if it's worth it."

Stasia moved away from Mac and toward the driver's door of the vehicle, motioning for the former Navy SEAL to get in.

"I have to be on the first morning flight back to Rome, Mr. Walker. I have a suite at the Hay-Adams, right above the *Off the Record*. Care to join me?"

Mac Walker looked across the roof of the sedan at the beautiful Stasia, and then glanced behind him toward the massive, five sided Pentagon building, a portion of which was still undergoing construction following last year's September 11th terrorist attack.

Inside that structure, Mac knew the machinations of many were colliding with the counter plans of others, and within that conflict, he would find himself playing some part in his new role as a Project Icon operative.

Life, as they say, was about to get complicated…

Epilogue:

The lamb stew was, as always, quite delicious, its thick hot juice running down the colonel's chin. Even during an early Zarzis evening such as this, with temperatures persisting in being uncomfortably warm, Colonel Mabazza made certain to introduce himself to the night with a customary bowl of stew, and at least one bottle of deep red wine brought up from the luxury, beachfront hotel's two thousand square foot wine cellar.

It had been nearly two years since he last visited his ancestral home in southeast Tunisia, the idyllic, warm breezed place that formed a happy and content childhood most in this nation of corruption and radicalized politics, would have thought impossible.

Colonel Mabazza had always led a charmed life, and he intended to keep it that way. More stew, more wine, more pleasures of the flesh, and more power of course. It was what Allah wished for him, of that, Mabazza was certain.

So let his enemies gnash their teeth back in the capitol of Tunis. They were not his betters – far from it. His military would keep him safe, as they had always done. Even in the face of accusations of wrongdoing involving that damn passenger plane, or his alleged allegiance to the Saudis, none of it would stop his quest for more power.

The boy looked increasingly frightened, the tears of earlier still wet on his cheeks. Good, that made the act so much more enjoyable, even if it was to be the second time in the last few hours. The child had been delivered to Mabazza's room with the promise of having not yet seen twelve summers.

Ah, the perfect age then – such sweet, delicious distraction.

How many such boys had he broken over the years? Was it yet a thousand?

The colonel's glass was emptied as he issued himself a silent toast.

Here's to a thousand more, Allah willing!

"Boy, get more wine from the kitchen, next to the sink. And hurry!"

Colonel Mabazza's eyes followed the boy's movement from the hotel bedroom to the kitchen, pleased with how the young body moved as he scampered away.

Yes, a thousand more just like that one…

The wine was late in coming, stirring anger within the colonel, a man unaccustomed to waiting for anyone or anything.

"Boy! What keeps you? My wine! My wine, and then I wash it down with more of you!"

Where is the wretched child?

The colonel rose naked from the large bed that dominated the hotel bedroom, and made his way angrily to the hallway, his bare feet slapping across the marble tiled floor.

"Such a naughty thing, eh? In need of some good punishment then! To hell with the wine, I will first deal with---"

Cold metal firmly pressed itself against the colonel's right temple. He knew instantly it was a gun.

"Hello, Colonel."

Colonel Mabazza froze, recognizing the tone of the voice indicated someone well versed in the ways of killing others.

"I'm afraid you have me at a disadvantage. You seem to know me, but I don't believe I know you."

The gun was jammed into the side of the colonel's head with even greater force.

"You shout, or try anything to piss me off, and you die sooner rather than later, understand?"

Though Colonel Mabazza maintained a calm exterior, his mind was racing for a way to escape, the panic welling up within him. He wondered it someone in the government had sent some assassin to eliminate him.

If that was the case though, wouldn't I already be dead?

Whoever the man with the gun to his head was, he seemed to want something. The colonel knew that wanting gave him some bit of leverage. Hopefully it would be enough to keep him alive.

"Over to the bed and sit down. And remember, no bullshit, or I shoot you dead."

Colonel Mabazza sat down once again on the hotel room bed, and was grateful to be able to look back at his would be killer. The man was of average height, clean shaven, with short cropped, slightly receding brown hair. He appeared to be a year or two shy of forty, with broad shoulders, lean hips, and an overall athletic, powerful build. The eyes were perhaps the man's most striking feature. They had a flinty, almost savage nature to them, like an alpha predator from the wild.

The colonel had no idea who the man was, having never seen him before.

"May I ask who you are?"

The weapon remained trained on the colonel's head.

"I was a passenger on a certain flight back from Paris recently."

It is the one Huskich called army boy! The one who killed several of my men!

"Ah, I see. Well, that was an unfortunate thing. A…misunderstanding. I did not know what was intended, and was happy to see the whole thing prevented before many more came to harm."

The man shook his head and smirked, the look causing the colonel to forget the weapon pointed at him, his indignation momentarily overcoming his fear.

"You find that funny?"

The man shrugged.

"Yeah, I suppose I do. Seems no matter where I go, a politician always sounds like a politician. Lying sacks of useless shit, saying whatever needs to be said to save their own ass."

Colonel Mabazza's mouth extended into a thin, pained smile.

"For an American, your Arabic is excellent."

The man's eyes narrowed as his trigger finger tightened ever so slightly.

"And for a monster, you almost resemble something human."

The colonel's smile disappeared.

"What do you want army boy? Why this game? If you have come to kill me, why not be done with it?"

The man issued a soft grunt.

"Normally, you would be dead without an introduction, but I want information. The more you have to say, the longer you live."

Colonel Mabazza tried hard not to appear overly pleased. It was the very answer he was hoping for, confirming he did in fact hold some leverage over the visiting killer.

"Well then, I guess that makes me a very willing informant for you. Please, ask your questions."

The man lowered his gun, but the eyes remained locked and loaded.

"Why would you be part of an attack on the Vatican? The others had motive. They were radicalized, survivors of a conflict drenched in the blood of Catholics and Muslims killing one another. But why you? What would motivate you to take on such a risk? You're clearly no Islamic fundamentalist. So why attack Rome?"

The colonel rolled his eyes and shrugged, attempting to appear disinterested in the question.

"Why not? I have no love of the infidels. I may not be your version of a Muslim, but I am Muslim nevertheless, and ten or twenty thousand fewer Catholics on this earth, is nothing more to me than a good start."

The man raised his gun again, and prepared to shoot.

"You try and bullshit me like that again, and this conversation is over, and that means your brains are left all over that wall behind you."

Colonel Mabazza held up both his hands, each of which was noticeably shaking. When he spoke again, he did so in perfect English.

"Ok, ok! Let me try again!"

The colonel was pleased to see a hint of surprise cross over the man's face.

"Yes, my English is even better than your Arabic. Now why is that do you suppose? You come in here, waiving that gun at me, demanding answers, but I am nothing more than a middle man! If you kill me, you are simply chopping off the little toe of a much larger foot, one that will crush you underneath its heel."

"So who do *you* answer to, Colonel?"

Colonel Mabazza's eyes lit up with mischievous glee as he pointed back at the armed man come to kill him.

"It is very likely the same people *you* answer to, army boy. Eventually, it all connects somewhere. There is wonderfully terrible change coming – so very quickly now! Those towers coming down was but the signal, a candle of hope that has been the too long darkness. Already your country hungers for more war, destruction, revenge. First is Afghanistan, but you won't stop there, will you? Then Iraq, long the enemy of both Iran, and the House of Saud. Perhaps not long after, so too will Libya be transformed. And why not Syria too while you're at it? Revenge breeds wars upon wars, funded by borrowed money you can never hope to repay, while enemies pretend friendship, and wait until the inevitable fall.

"But do not look to me as an agent of that downfall army boy. No, the knife will be held by one who claims to be among you. His place at the head of the table is already being set. The great wound will be self inflicted, deep, and irreversible.

"The blood will flow, America will fall, AND-WE-WILL-WIN."

The gun was once again raised, and then pressed against the colonel's temple, a curious smile the armed man's only initial response to the colonel's rant regarding his hoped for end to America.

"You know what you call the death of just one lunatic, Third World tyrant with allusions of grandeur and a sickness for raping young boys?"

Before Colonel Mabazza had a chance to respond, a single bullet entered through his right temple, fracturing skull bone, searing a trench through brain, and then leaving a fist sized exit would out of which several handfuls of mottled blood and gray matter exploded against the wall behind him.

As Mac Walker watched the colonel's already dead body fall backwards onto the bed, he snarled the answer to his own question.

"A damn good start."

END.

**CHECK OUT D.W. ULSTERMAN'S
LATEST NOVELS!**

He gave his word, refused to break a vow, and lost his one chance at true love.

Now they've come for his land.

Hap Wilkes is a man facing a painful past, an increasingly uncertain future, and now fights with everything left in a broken and failing body to keep the one thing still left to him – his pride.

The Irish Cowboy is a story of loss, secrets, redemption, and the always present human yearning for love and forgiveness, and marks the most personal novel to date from bestselling author D.W. Ulsterman.

"If you love the concept of a Free America, and those few left who have the TRUE pioneer spirit, and a tender love story - READ this book!" -Hercy A. Lord

All novels available at Amazon.com

ABOUT THE AUTHOR:

D.W. Ulsterman lives near his beloved waters with his beautiful wife of 22 years, and their two teenage children, along with two cats and two dogs.

His interests, beyond the always-present task of writing, are music, film, fishing, an often infuriating golf game, respectable BBQ skills, and sampling various wines from around the world. He feels blessed to share his days with the love of his life, and watch their two children grow into the remarkable young adults they have become.

Many of D.W. Ulsterman's personal interests are reflected in his works, including a love of America, classic rock, and the "indelible education that results from experiencing fist to face."

His writings include the bestselling Mac Walker series of books, including the epic tales DOMINATUS and TUMULTUS, as well as the more recent Bennington P.I. series.

This past summer he released his most personal novel to date, **The Irish Cowboy.**

Please visit D.W. Ulsterman at his website **ulstermanbooks.com** and sign up for his newsletter to receive timely updates and special deals available only to his subscribers.

Printed in Great Britain
by Amazon